LIFE WITH A
PSYCHOPATH

FRANCESCA DI PIETRO

Published in Australia by Sid Harta Books & Print Pty Ltd,
ABN: 34632585293
23 Stirling Crescent, Glen Waverley, Victoria 3150 Australia
Telephone: +61 3 9560 9920
E-mail: author@sidharta.com.au

First published in Australia 2022
This edition published 2022
Copyright © Francesca Di Pietro 2022
Cover design, typesetting: WorkingType (www.workingtype.com.au)

Di Pietro , Francesca
Life with a Psychopath
ISBN: 978-1-925707-71-7
pp256

ABOUT THE AUTHOR

FRANCESCA DI PIETRO was born and raised in Melbourne where she continues to reside with her family. Francesca completed her Bachelor of Arts Degree with majors in Professional Writing and Editing and Communication Studies. By day, she works as an administrator with the Victorian State Government.

Francesca has a passion for storytelling, especially tales which highlight the dark side of human nature, manipulative and aberrant behaviour. Francesca is a night writer which is when her creativity shines. *Life with a Psychopath* is her first full length novel.

*Dedicated to victims/survivors
of the rooster smashers of this world*

PROLOGUE

My name is Carmella and this is my story. I had a pretty good childhood despite the constant bullying and racism directed towards me. To put this into context, I have an Italian background which wasn't an advantage in late twentieth century Australia, and if that wasn't enough, I was considered to be the fat kid at school as well. In fact, I was the second fattest kid in the class after a boy. How embarrassing was that for a poor little girl? Those were the worst situations I had to battle through as a child and they have left me emotionally scarred to this day. I do, however, believe I have successfully overcome a lot of the trauma but won't ever forget some of the things that happened to me. I'm a big believer in not forgetting how others treat you whether it's good or bad.

Life dramatically improved for me once I 'found my

people' at university. Suddenly, I discovered people who thought like me and enjoyed the things I liked. We had so much in common, including the clubs we often visited right down to our Friday night pool games at the local sports bar. Thankfully, I still remain friends with a lot of the people I met there. I also lost what my mother referred to as seventeen years of 'puppy fat'. I rose to my full height of five feet ten inches, and became tall and leggy. My eyes also found a certain sparkle I never even realised they possessed. I had definitely found my edge, and the confidence which accompanied that was life changing.

After successfully completing my Masters degree in Event Management, I went on to work with a company who specialised in the running of student events, appropriately named Student Glamour. I fell into event management by chance, but it totally suited my personality as I have always been organised and love to work at a very rapid pace. Most of my work experiences at this company have definitely been positive with the exception of one horrific experience which my book details.

My parents, especially my father, cherished me and my older siblings, Isabella and Stefano. We didn't have a lot of money but we always had a roof over our head and food to eat which was all that mattered. Family life was always pretty good and still is to this day. Being close-knit was always very important to me and to other members of my family. Sounds pretty normal so far, right? It's about to get juicier.

When you're young, it is almost every little girl's dream

to find their Prince Charming. Many women believe that there is one man for them who they will marry, have children and live happily ever after with. When I first met Shaun, I felt like I had finally met someone I could discover a real connection with. Charming, tall, attractive and intelligent, he seemed to have it all. After a number of attempts in trying to find a relationship, I felt as though I had struck gold and it was about time too! This unfortunately wasn't the case. What started off as one of the best things that ever happened to me very quickly evaporated to become one of the worst. The sad part about it was that for the majority of the relationship, I knew what was happening but chose to ignore it. I also kept a lot of what was happening to me a secret. There were many reasons for this, including that I wanted everyone to think I was happy, and I was also embarrassed to admit what was going on. In the eyes of my friends and family, I was always known to be opinionated and one to call out bad behaviour if it was wrong. The prime reason for keeping this secret however was that I was just plain scared. If I left, what would he do to me? What would he do to my family and friends? Even if I left, would I ever be free of him? In my experience, leaving an abusive relationship is one of the scariest things you'll ever have to encounter and for some it may even feel like your life isn't worth living. You will become so involved and invested, regardless of the circumstances, that the only thing in your life that matters is protecting your relationship. Unlike me, if this ever happens to you, be sure to tell someone. You could tell a family member, friend, work colleague or resort to one of the many forms of support services available to all nowadays.

I have written this book for the female population out there. It is important to me that you all hear my story and then make a decision on whether the one you're with is the one you want to spend the rest of your life with. Ask yourself these few questions:

Does it feel right?

Are you happy?

Do you ever feel frightened in any way?

Do you feel as though your life is no longer yours?

If you have answered 'no' to the first two questions and 'yes' to the last two (even if your answer is 'only sometimes') you probably need to look more closely at your relationship. Love between two people should be calming and soothing. It should be a bond which you're certain cannot break, or that you don't want to be broken. Most of all though, the person you've chosen to be with should be easy to be around. You should be comfortable being yourself around them at all times. Tragically, the relationship I describe in this book was not at all like that. I look back upon this time of my life with sadness but I'm happy I can tell you all about it. Don't get me wrong, there were some good times, but the time I spent with Shaun went on for a lot longer than it should have. I saw the warning signs and did not act quickly enough for a number of reasons.

The feeling of being able to share my story is amazing

and in fact quite liberating. I feel as though I am no longer withholding this tale as mine alone.

I am hoping this book will assist in helping, supporting and informing others but that you will also find the story interesting at the same time. This relationship felt like one long nightmare and I still often dream that I am back, stuck in this situation. A sense of relief washes over me every time I wake up from these dreams. I remained traumatised long after it ended and it took me a great deal of time to learn to trust again and to allow anybody to get close to me.

It is important to me that I can help to prevent other women from suffering as I did. I will be happy if my story encourages even one victim to leave a relationship of domestic violence, verbal and emotional abuse.

Lots of people say that there are two sides to every story, so here is mine.

Enjoy, love Carmella x

CHAPTER 1
THE MEETING

'I need a drink,' I said to Sarah as we walked into the karaoke bar. It had been a rough day at work for me. My team at the event management company had finished organising yet another successful project. I absolutely loved my work and sometimes even the stress that came with it. Student Glamour, the private company I was employed by, ran events and conferences which aimed to assist university students, particularly those with special needs. It was a great cause and I believed in the goals of the company which is what made me love my line of work even more.

Arriving at the bar to buy my well-earned alcoholic beverage, I stopped dead in my tracks when I first saw him. Blonde-haired, blue-eyed, he was over six feet tall and wearing blue jeans with a red shirt. He was just walking off the karaoke stage. I couldn't help noticing the silver stud he wore in his left ear also. There was a large group of people which greeted him as he stepped off, both male and female. I wondered what song he had finished singing. I had been so focussed on getting a drink that I hadn't even been listening to the music. He noticed me looking at him, paused and then gave me a cheeky grin. I smiled back, grabbed the drinks I ordered and hurried back to Sarah and the girls.

'Who's that?' Sarah asked, pointing to the guy I was eyeing off. 'I caught the intense stare you both gave one another.'

I told her I wasn't sure and tried changing the subject. The attraction I felt towards him was very strong but I thought he looked way out of my league. He probably had women swooning over him all the time. Coming from an Italian background, life had never been easy for me. Growing up, I was always the object of racial taunts and remarks which still scarred me. Constantly fighting with my weight was also a huge challenge for me and still was to some extent. Once you have been overweight, the self-consciousness of this and the negative body image remains with you forever.

'Oh my God, he's coming over here,' Sarah said excitedly.

I didn't have time to utter a reply before he had reached us. He was even better looking close up. My heart started to pound very quickly. Did my hair look OK? Did my breath smell? All the answers to these questions didn't matter as he was actually standing there now.

'How are you ladies?' he asked us, mainly looking at me. 'Do you sing?'

I really could not get over that smile. Sarah started to respond but his eyes never left me. She noticed where his eyes were focused and quickly zipped her mouth.

'Good thanks,' I replied softly looking down at my drink. 'No, singing is definitely not my thing.'

I felt like sculling the entire contents of what was in my glass. This situation came very unexpectedly. The last time I had even spoken to a guy while being out was quite some time ago. It had in fact ended in a disaster when the guy I was chatting to expected me to go home with him that night. I don't judge women who do that thing but it's not my scene.

We got chatting and I was surprised at how easily the conversation flowed. The guy's name was Shaun. He told me what a fantastic night he was having and how happy he was to be out and about. I realised that nearly half an hour had passed when I told Shaun I had better go and spend time with Sarah and the other girls I came to the bar with. He asked if he could have my number and I agreed. This situation was moving very fast for me.

The girls were all looking at me in anticipation as I walked back over to them.

'How did you go?' Belinda, a friend of mine, asked excitedly. 'He's so hot.'

I told them Shaun and I had a good chat and he got my number. The girls were so excited except for Sarah who seemed a little reserved. When the other girls went to the bar for another round of drinks, I stayed behind with Sarah and asked her if everything was OK.

'There's something a little off about Shaun but I can't quite put my finger on it,' she said. 'I got this weird feeling when he walked over to us and started talking.'

I was a little surprised at Sarah's quick judgement as she was usually the type of person who liked everybody. Could it be because he wanted to talk to me and not to her? This wasn't a conversation to get into at this particular moment, so I thought I'd keep it for a later stage.

The girls and I were about to leave the karaoke bar when Shaun must've spotted me. He asked me if I was able to stay behind for a further chat. Sarah, who rode with me, told me that Belinda could drop her home at the double storey unit we both lived in.

Shaun and I chatted further for a little while. Talkative and friendly, Shaun was about the most charismatic guy I had ever met. He was from an Irish background, worked full time in a bank and was also a business analyst by trade. I kept thinking about how much I would love to see him again to see what came out of it. He seemed so genuine and a bit cheeky at the same time, which was why I was so attracted to him.

When the night came to an end, Shaun walked me to my car, opened the door for me and waved goodbye. I was smitten by him which certainly came as a surprise to me. The fact that he admitted to singing 'Material Girl' by Madonna was also a bonus as I absolutely love her music.

The next morning I woke up to the beep of my phone.

It was Shaun. Wow, he was extremely interested, I thought to myself. The text said that he had a great time chatting with me last night and how much he was looking forward to seeing me again. I jumped out of bed and danced a little jig before heading into the kitchen to chat with Sarah.

'Hey, good morning,' I said to Sarah who was sitting at the table reading her horoscope prediction in the daily newspaper.

Sarah was big on astrology and religiously read her horoscope in the newspaper every day. She was a Scorpio and whilst always friendly, she was also cautious and suspicious of people at the same time. I was keen to talk more to Sarah regarding her initial thoughts about Shaun.

'Hi,' she said. 'How did you go last night?' Sarah looked up from the newspaper.

Knowing Sarah's first reaction to Shaun, I tried to reply in a cautious and casual manner.

'We had a good chat and I think I may see him again,' I replied. 'He has already texted me this morning too.'

'Isn't that a little soon?' Sarah asked.

I absolutely adored Sarah and she had been a big part of my life since we were children, despite attending separate schools. However, I was determined not to let her ruin my happy mood that morning. Sarah, knowing me so well, must've sensed that I was not going to get into a debate over Shaun.

'Look Carmella, I know you're keen and I am happy for you,' she said. 'All I am asking is that you take it slow and be careful.'

Sarah had always looked out for me and I often found myself thinking about how grateful I was to have her in my life. I did however feel she was being a bit overprotective about the whole thing.

'Sarah! It's only a date,' I laughed.

I was secretly more excited about seeing Shaun than I let on. It was the most excited I'd felt for quite some time.

CHAPTER 2

FIRST DATE

Over the next couple of days, I continued to talk to Shaun. I found him to be a little full on but I have frequently been told that I am quick to judge. He was always full of compliments which included telling me how beautiful and intelligent I was. I'd only met him once and found myself thinking he was going a little overboard. I was not the best at accepting compliments and always found them to be awkward. This is what happens as the result of being bullied as a child. However, after a while I began to relax and took everything he said in. Despite the niggling little doubts within me, I said 'yes' to going out on a date. I was excited about seeing him again. If I didn't go, I would always wonder what would've happened. Besides, meeting someone in person is a much better way of making the decision than over the phone.

We decided to do something casual and go for a stroll in the shopping centre. Something romantic on the first date would've put me off. Shaun insisted on buying me this stunning dress I'd been eyeing in the window of a fancy boutique. The dress was gorgeous but I could've lived without it, especially when so many people were starving out there. After several attempts at trying to decline Shaun's offer, I ended up having to give in. The last thing I wanted was an embarrassing situation. The dress was expensive and was nothing I could ever afford.

Once I was dragged inside by Shaun, the shop assistant brought out two different colours telling me that the blue one would look stunning with my luscious curves. Shaun immediately got angry as he felt that the shop assistant was calling me fat. I had experienced people being rude on a number of occasions and this certainly wasn't one of them. I honestly didn't mind and wasn't hurt or upset by this at all and I expressed this to Shaun, but he didn't seem to listen to my words at all. He told the sales assistant to get some manners and to stop being insulting. I blushed with embarrassment as other shoppers looked on. Shaun told me he didn't want to be seen in a place where people discriminated against others. He handed me money for the dress before walking out of the shop. After Shaun was out of sight, I apologised to the sales assistant.

'I'm really sorry,' I said to her. 'I didn't expect that to happen.'

I tried on the two dresses, one in blue and the other in yellow. The one I ended up purchasing was the yellow even though I actually favoured the blue. The colour honestly did bring out my curves. I thought it best to not go with the recommendation of the sales assistant.

When I walked out of the shop, I asked Shaun what was wrong and why he reacted that way. His face darkened with anger and he told me he didn't like to see me belittled by anybody. Shaun's behaviour in my opinion was extremely unjust and over the top. Having said this, however, it was nice to see that he was looking out for me in every way. This was me trying to see the positive side to Shaun's reaction. I had never had someone do this for me before. Not wanting to tell Shaun I didn't agree with his behaviour, I suggested that we see a movie. He was happy with this idea and we agreed on a new thriller movie we'd both been dying to see.

On arriving at the movie theatre, we stood in line to buy our tickets and some popcorn. We then walked into the theatre and took our seats. I started talking to Shaun and didn't realise the movie had started until a man behind me asked me if I could keep my voice down. The man was extremely polite but once again Shaun got very angry about the whole thing. With an expression of pure rage, he angrily told the man to shift seats if he wasn't happy. I tried to enjoy the movie but for the second time that day was so embarrassed by Shaun's actions. What a short fuse this man had! This somehow wasn't the vibe I was expecting on our first date.

After the movie, we decided to wander to a nearby Italian restaurant for dinner. I knew the place very well and was secretly praying that Shaun wouldn't cause a scene of chaos there. Shaun's behaviour had been absolutely terrible all day so I couldn't help feeling concerned. I made the decision that if I was at all uncomfortable during dinner then I would not see Shaun again. This was his absolute last chance. We had only ever seen each other twice so nobody's heart was going to get broken this early on.

When we got to the restaurant, a waiter I knew well showed us to my favourite table next to an open window. The evening breeze was wonderful so it was the perfect table. We carefully ordered drinks and our meals as everything listed on the menu looked delicious. Shaun smiled and told me that he was very impressed by the level of treatment in this restaurant. We laughed and joked throughout the whole meal as we ate our delectable food. I started to relax as our date dramatically improved. Shaun started talking about things we would do in the future together which made me start to think that maybe I would see him again. After the waiter brought us our dessert of Tiramisu and the bill, we wandered back to Shaun's car and he insisted on driving me home.

The second half of our date together had been wonderful. Shaun and I had a great conversation on the drive back home to my place.

'I'm really sorry about what happened in the clothes shop and the movie theatre,' Shaun said.

I found myself thinking this to be a highly promising sign. Shaun had obviously realised that his behaviour was out of line and I was truly grateful for his apology.

'It's OK,' I replied. 'Everyone loses their cool sometimes.'

'I really care about you Carmella and don't want anybody to ever treat you badly,' Shaun replied.

I was touched by Shaun's words. He seemed to greatly care about me already. Could this be the type of relationship I'd been looking for if I stopped being cynical and just gave it a chance? Shaun continued to drive as he launched into a torrent of lovely words about me and how he was starting to feel.

'I want to continue seeing you and see how it goes,' Shaun continued. 'I feel a real connection with you.'

No man had ever come onto me this strong and so soon. Could it be that nobody ever felt the way Shaun did about me?

Shaun pulled into my driveway when we got to my place and stopped the car. He then leaned in so close to me that I could feel his warm breath on my right cheek. He turned my face towards his for a slow and deep kiss. Once finished, he jumped out the door from his side of the car so he could open mine for me. He promised to call me and drove off. I was left wanting more.

CHAPTER 3
SECOND DATE

After our first date, Shaun and I began chatting almost every day. We were in frequent contact whether it was by phone call, text or email. Shaun revealed a lot more about his job at the bank and also his love of data analysis and programming. I was so excited when Shaun suggested that we see each other again. Following the hiccups of our first date, I wanted to see Shaun for another date to find out if something could develop further. More importantly, I also wanted to look out for further strange behaviours I needed to be aware of. I found I was most impressed by his future ambitions and career choices. He wasn't simply another handsome guy and this fact drew me in even more. Intelligence was always an important trait for me in a man.

Shaun suggested we go out for dinner on our second

date. That suited me just fine as I was keen to find out more about him and it gave us a chance to talk. Shaun wanted to pick me up but I told him I would meet him there instead which he was cool with. We arranged to meet at 7.00 pm at the Hard Rock Café. This venue was fun and bustling which was the exact vibe I wanted for our night out. They also had a band and we both loved music so it was perfect.

When I arrived there, Shaun was already waiting for me. He looked immaculate in a dark pair of jeans and black shirt which brought out the blue colour of his eyes. I decided to wear the dress he had purchased for me on our previous date. Shaun told me I looked beautiful as he took my hand and we walked inside. He had such an air of confidence which was one of the many things I liked about him. We took a seat in a booth and spent the next couple of hours constantly chatting over burgers and fries.

After we finished eating, I suggested that we walk over and enjoy the band. To my disappointment, Shaun announced that he had to go as he had an early start in the morning. I tried not to let my feelings show as I gathered up my bag and Shaun fixed up the bill.

Afterwards, Shaun insisted on walking me to the train station even though I said I'd be fine.

'I had a very nice time,' I told Shaun when we reached my train platform.

'I did too and sorry for cutting it short,' Shaun replied.

As my train approached, Shaun kissed me a second time which once again caused fireworks. I boarded the train and took a seat. As I started to think about when to next contact Shaun, I heard my phone beep. It was a text from Shaun reiterating what a great time he had with me. I was still in business.

Shaun contacted me the next day and after that we went on a couple more dates which went extremely well. He then suggested that I go to his house that weekend for dinner and drinks. I accepted without a moment's hesitation. Sarah, having met Shaun again when dropping by our place to pick me up for a previous date, said she was still picking up negative vibes about him. I blocked out her comments and tried to enjoy my newfound happiness. She didn't have a proper explanation for her feelings which made it extremely difficult for me to understand.

It had been quite some time since I had been invited to a man's house for dinner. I was awfully nervous about everything including what to wear, how to act and if Shaun would expect sex. Trying to push all these thoughts out of my mind I started to get ready for my outing. I decided on a pair of jeans and a top. I didn't feel the need to go overboard as it was dinner at his place. Squirting a spray of my favourite perfume, I excitedly left the house.

When I arrived at Shaun's place, I wasn't expecting it to be so new, big and spacious. He told me to take a walk around while he tended to the finishing touches of the beautiful roast lamb dinner he had cooked up. He was a brilliant cook on top of everything else! I took a look at some of the photographs he had on his lounge room mantelpiece. There were a lot of framed pictures of his parents and siblings which told me that he was close to his family. A photo of himself and his mother was prominently displayed in the centre of the mantelpiece. Both were smiling and Shaun had his arm around her. They looked identical. I took Shaun's affection for his mother as a good sign. I wondered if I'd ever get to meet her. Before I could look any further, Shaun announced that dinner was ready. We sat down to enjoy the delicious meal over a glass of wine and talked non-stop. Afterwards, we settled down on his lounge room couch to watch a horror movie. Shaun knew horror was my favourite film genre as it had come up in conversation quite a number of times. We didn't get too far into the film as we continued talking and it felt like we could keep going forever. I told Shaun some of my deepest and darkest secrets including stories of racism and bullying for being overweight which I had encountered a lot in my life.

'You'll never have to worry about anything like that when you're around me,' Shaun said. 'I will always protect you.'

At that moment all I felt was emotional attachment for this man even though I hardly knew him. I wondered if this was at all possible.

'I feel so protected around you,' I replied.

Shaun leant in to softly kiss me which quickly turned deep and lustful. I felt an explosion deep inside of me which I had never before experienced. Shaun grabbed my hand and led me into his bedroom. We made passionate love all night long. It all happened so naturally and felt so right.

It was late morning when I awoke from a deep sleep. Shaun wasn't in bed next to me but I could smell freshly brewed coffee coming from the kitchen. I put on one of Shaun's robes which I found hooked up on his bedroom door and made my way to the kitchen.

'Good morning,' Shaun said, smiling brightly at me.

I smiled back and stared at him. I could not believe my luck. He was just so damn gorgeous.

'Good morning,' I replied. 'Thanks again for dinner and now breakfast I see.'

Shaun walked towards me and embraced me. Slowly he let go and looked into my eyes.

'Look Carmella, I am going to say this outright,' Shaun started. 'I had a great time last night and I like you a lot. I'm not sure how you feel but all I know is that I want to start seeing you exclusively and nobody else.'

From then on, I knew I was all his, whether my mind was made up or not.

CHAPTER 4
MOVING IN TOGETHER

'I think we should move in together,' Shaun said one warm and sunny afternoon.

We were sitting across from one another in one of our favourite cafes, both sipping on lattes. The place was bustling and I thought I might have misheard what Shaun said until he repeated himself again. I looked into my glass and studied the colour of my drink. The colour of a latte had never been of interest to me until this point. I'd been drinking this brown murky liquid for years. I slowly put my drink down and tried to digest what Shaun had suggested. In my mind I was thinking it may be a little too soon. Did I really know Shaun that well? I rapidly pushed my thoughts away, thinking I was sometimes way too cautious. We had only been seeing each other for two months but I convinced myself that this was the happiest

I had ever been in my life. Since that disastrous first date everything was going swimmingly well. Why try to stop happiness if everything was working and felt right?

Back and forth we had conversations about whose place we should move into. We decided on Shaun's as his was more spacious and he lived alone. The last thing I wanted to do was leave poor Sarah, who I already knew would be homeless and unhappy with my decision. I told him I couldn't wait to move in with him, not knowing myself if those words were true or not. Having said this though, being with another person was something I yearned for. Shaun seemed like he deeply cared for me and I loved being around him. After a number of bad experiences, I thought it would be nice to have those feelings of affection and security back in my life. And besides, if it didn't work out for us I always had the option of leaving. I wasn't a prisoner in my own life. This was the first time I would be living alone together with a man. Surely this was something I should be excited about?

When I told Sarah the news, I can't say she was overly surprised or impressed. The reaction was one I totally expected. Her face dropped and she avoided eye contact with me. I wished she would have been happy for me.

'Come on Sarah! I so want to do this,' I said to her. 'We'll still see each other a lot and you know you can stay in my townhouse as long as you need to.'

Sarah had continued to warn me time and time again that there was something about Shaun which wasn't quite right. 'I can't quite put my finger on it,' she would repeatedly say. I shook my head and replied that with no evidence or examples she should not be making those remarks. Shaun had also made such an effort with Sarah by coming over with yummy takeaway meals and taking us to the movies. I ignored her words while still keeping them in the back of my mind.

When it was time, Sarah begrudgingly helped me pack my belongings. She gave me a long, compassionate hug on my way out the door and held me for longer than she usually would. I couldn't help thinking at that point that she was being a bit of a drama queen. Shaun's house was a twenty minute drive from ours. Sarah behaved like I would never see her again.

It was the Queen's Birthday long weekend when I moved into Shaun's place. I had engaged a moving company headed by Sarah's brother, Alan, to move a lot of my belongings to what would be my new home. I had known Alan as long as I had known Sarah. We all grew up together and spent so much time with each other's families. Alan was like a brother to me. He had been there through all the ups and downs in my life including all my failed relationships. Unlike his sister, Alan was extremely happy that I had found happiness with Shaun.

The movers were intrigued by my extensive book and DVD movie collection as everybody was. I still hadn't gotten into kindles or pay TV.

'I can see that you packed every movie from your massive DVD collection,' Alan said, peering into the clear boxes the movies were stored in. He opened one of the boxes and picked up a copy of the original *A Nightmare on Elm Street*.

'I most certainly did,' I replied. 'As you can see, all my horror movies are there, especially my favourite.' I pointed to the movie he was holding in his hand.

'I remember when you and Sarah used to have slumber parties at my parents' house and watch movies,' Alan replied and laughed. 'That seems like such a long time ago now.'

I laughed back, raising my arms and yawning at the same time. 'Sorry, moving always makes me tired.'

The moving company finished their job and left for the day. It was at that point when things unexpectedly took a turn for the worse.

Shaun began to give me the silent treatment as soon as we were alone. This was the quietest I had ever seen him. I asked him if everything was OK and in reply got a quick 'I'm fine.' We spent most of our time apart that afternoon which left me to stew alone with my thoughts. Why could Shaun possibly be so unhappy? I thought me moving in with him was what he wanted. Was he having second thoughts? Had I done something wrong? Did I say something out of line? If so, I was totally unaware of what that might be. These were all the questions which were racing through my mind. Even though I desperately wanted answers, I made a decision to leave Shaun alone. I felt a bit uncomfortable that I had just moved in with him and we couldn't be honest about our feelings. I sincerely hoped that this wasn't a taste of how issues to come would be handled.

I didn't have to wait long to find out Shaun's reason for cracking it. Shaun's problem came out when we were seated and eating the delicious roast chicken dinner I'd prepared for our first night living together. I thought it would be a nice touch to prepare something special.

'You know what you did, don't you?' Shaun asked me.

I looked up from my dinner and slowly shook my head in reply. There it was, I had done something wrong and was undoubtedly about to find out what.

'I know you were flirting with the men from the moving company,' continued Shaun. 'You also yawned and lifted your arms so they could check out your boobs.'

I dropped my fork on my plate, my appetite had suddenly disappeared. This was absolutely absurd and extremely laughable at the same time. I started to defend myself, trying to contain the feelings of shock I had experienced.

'Shaun, what are you talking about?' I asked. 'I would never do anything like that. Alan is like a brother to me and I have known him for most of my life. It upsets me to think you would even believe I would do something like that. What a crazy thought.'

I then went on to say that maybe we moved in together too quickly and suggested that I leave. Following an extensive debate, Shaun talked me into staying and made me promise not to do anything like that again. I promised what was asked of me, but hearing myself say those words of agreement made me feel so ridiculous. Could I guarantee that I wouldn't lift my arms up and yawn in front of men? He then took me into his arms and kissed me which once again filled me with hope but I also had doubts at the same time. I tried to convince myself that he may have been right. My mind however did not allow me to believe that.

CHAPTER 5
MEETING MY FAMILY

The first time Shaun met my family was at a New Year's Eve barbecue. We spent the day in bed before making our way to my family's place that evening. My immediate family consisted of my parents, brother and sister, not to mention partners and children, aunts, uncles and cousins included in the mix. I was the youngest out of my brother and sister which made my family even more protective of me. In attendance at the barbecue would also be my extended family including siblings of my father as well as my cousins. I was a little nervous about the event but Shaun didn't seem to be. This put me at ease a little. He was probably used to everybody liking him so found a lot of enjoyment at these social gatherings. I, for one can be a little socially awkward and always feel pangs of anxiety before any interaction with people. My family can be a little loud and boisterous at times so I thought that Shaun would fit right in with their playfulness.

When we arrived there I introduced Shaun to my parents. My parents were a little reserved to begin with but then they slowly began to open up. It had been quite a while since they had seen me with a man. Shaun's easy-going composure seemed to provide a relaxed vibe and conversation began from there. Eventually as the night progressed, I could see there was a lot of banter between my parents, sister, brother, cousins and Shaun. It seemed he had won quite a few of the family members over, which was great. Even cousin Antonio, the family's recluse, seemed to take a liking to Shaun. I found it entirely comforting as I saw Shaun involving Antonio in the conversation. He even put his arm around him in a couple of instances. Australian Rules football, as it frequently was, seemed to be a main topic of conversation. I tried not to hover as I didn't want to seem like I was Shaun's minder and I was also not a great fan of football. When I saw that Shaun was engrossed in conversation, I took the opportunity to have a proper chat with family members I had not caught up with in a while, particularly my cousin Lucia.

'How's it all going?' Lucia asked me. 'By the looks of things, you seem pretty well.'

I laughed at her comment. Being similar in age and personality, Lucia and I had always been close. I loved the fact that we could always be ourselves around one another and didn't take things too seriously. Married now with children, it was heartening to see that it had enhanced her positive and fun-loving attitude. She and I chatted for a while and she absolutely loved the story of how Shaun and I met.

'It's not often you meet good quality men in bars, especially karaoke ones,' Lucia said.

After the meal ended, everyone gathered in the lounge room to watch a movie. Shaun hugged and kissed me as we sat down together. There were a few positive glances coming our way. I think my feelings for Shaun were glaringly obvious. Also, there was no way I would've invited him to this gathering if I wasn't serious about him. After several attempts at trying to establish a long-term relationship with men I wasn't passionately interested in or vice versa, this was the first time I felt comfortable introducing Shaun to the family.

The end of the evening arrived and everything seemed to have gone very well which I was pleased to see. I also saw that Shaun had swapped emails and phone numbers with some of the family. Before we left for the evening, some family members came to tell me how much they liked Shaun, others didn't say anything. Should I have seen this as a sign of reserving judgement? Reassurance from others is one thing I have always liked to have, especially with people I cared about like my family. I tried not to read too much into the situation. People were busy talking and catching up throughout the night. It was probably one of the rare occasions people actually managed to see each other. And I also couldn't expect to be the main topic of everyone's conversations.

On the way home, Shaun told me he had a good time and liked most of the attendees at the gathering. This made me very happy. A rift this early into our relationship would have made things awkward. The compliments continued until he told me he didn't appreciate a comment my mother made about a conversation they were having about football. Shaun was a mad North Melbourne supporter as I found out on the night we met.

'Your mum said that the Richmond coach did a good job with the team this year,' Shaun said.

OK, I thought to myself, not exactly sure what he was getting at. I then asked him to continue.

'Richmond pretty much beat North Melbourne in every match this year,' Shaun continued. 'Was she saying that North Melbourne are a shit team?'

I told him I wasn't privy to the conversation so I wasn't overly sure. At the same time I found myself thinking what a bizarre issue to be raised after a fun evening. Knowing my mother, I was more than sure it was a throwaway comment. I tried to push my feelings of anxiety aside and asked Shaun what he would like me to do about it.

'Oh nothing babe,' Shaun said. 'I just thought you should know in case something like that happened again.'

Now I was slightly worried. Did this mean that I had to listen to all conversations Shaun was involved in? Also, how would I know what comments would upset him? My face must've worn some sort of weird look as Shaun tried to reassure me that everything was OK.

'Carmella, seriously, it's all fine,' Shaun said. 'Forget I said anything.'

We arrived back home right on time to welcome the New Year. I always loved the New Year as to me it was a symbol for starting afresh. I took a bottle of chilled champagne from the fridge and poured two glasses. At the stroke of midnight Shaun and I toasted to new beginnings. We also made a list of things we wanted to do together and achieve in the New Year. I found myself getting excited as we talked about some of the places we both wanted to visit which included Nepal, Spain, Egypt and of course the Amalfi Coast in Italy as Shaun had never been. By the end of it, the list was so extensive that I found myself thinking what a great and busy year we would both have. It was such a warm feeling knowing that I would have someone to spend the entire year with. The earlier events completely left my mind at that point. I fell asleep feeling blissfully happy in Shaun's arms which was right where I thought I wanted to be at the time.

CHAPTER 6
MONSTER MATT

I t had now been around three months since I'd moved in with Shaun. Things were going well and there had been no hiccups or issues since the New Year's Eve barbecue.

One afternoon, I found myself in the kitchen pondering what to cook for dinner. The doorbell rang when I was deciding between a roast chicken or stir fry. Running to the door, I answered it and a man I recognised, living a couple of doors away, stormed into the house. He demanded to know where Shaun was. I told him that he was not home but that I would tell him that he came past to see him. My heart was pounding as I asked the man his name. Instead of answering me he tramped through the entire household and yelled out that he was looking for something important belonging to him. When he seemed to have finished, I politely asked the man to leave. To my sheer relief he abruptly left and I quickly locked the door behind him. I then ran through the entire house ensuring that all doors and windows were locked. I remained on edge until Shaun arrived home. He obviously had some secrets which I intended to find out. I wondered if Shaun knew if this man was dangerous.

Shaun walked in at around 6 pm that evening and he looked angry. Before I could tell him the events of that afternoon, he informed me that the tyres of my car had been slashed. I hurriedly went on to explain what happened that afternoon. When I had finished telling my story, Shaun was absolutely furious. He explained that the man who lived a few doors down from us was someone named Matt. He and Matt went to school together and were friendly until Matt lapsed into serious drug addiction after his parents were killed in a car accident. In fact, Shaun had actually helped Matt pull himself together and get clean in an earlier, less serious bout of addiction. Then Shaun went on to explain that Matt was jealous of him because he had made a real life for himself. From Shaun's perspective, he had what Matt lacked: a supportive family, a successful career and a succession of women. I asked Shaun if he had any idea what Matt could have been looking for. The only reply I got was that my car now needed four new tyres. I totally understood and knew that, but it didn't answer the question I had asked.

The next day was Saturday and Shaun announced that he needed to go out. This caught me by surprise as Saturday was usually our day together. I asked him where he was going and he replied, 'Just dealing with some business.' Without another word, Shaun stormed off to have a shower. When I was headed back to the kitchen, I noticed that there were four white envelopes on the dining room table. I leant over to take a closer look at what was in them. They were thick and seemed to be filled with wads of cash. I didn't know what to think. Before Shaun left the house he picked up the envelopes and jammed them in his inner jacket pocket. I tried not to let what I saw play on my mind and thought instead of how I would spend the morning.

It was now a week later when Shaun asked if I could pick him up from work. I told him I could as I was lucky enough to have the day off. Before I left the house, I grabbed my bag, keys and phone and locked the door behind me. When I backed out of the driveway I saw that there was a big moving van at the house a few doors down from our place. When I observed more closely, I saw that it was Matt's place, lucky number seven. There were movers filling the van with Matt's things. What I saw next greatly disturbed me. Matt was on crutches, had his arm in a sling and his face was full of bruises. My mind was racing and I had a million questions. How did this happen? Who did this? I thought back to the events of last week including Matt storming into the house, Shaun's anger and the envelopes of cash. I decided it was time to ask Shaun what was going on.

Shaun was waiting for me as I zoomed up in front of the bank.

'Hi babe,' Shaun said.

'Hi,' I answered back as Shaun leant in to kiss me.

Things between us were going so well that I hated to ask about Matt but felt I had to.

'When coming to pick you up I noticed that Matt is moving,' I said. 'There was a van in front of his house. By the looks of things he's been beat up pretty badly.'

'Oh yeah,' Shaun said. 'It's about time that scumbag left the neighbourhood.'

'Do you know what happened to him?' I asked.

'No, why would I?' said Shaun.

'It happened straight after him storming into our house and my tyres being slashed,' I replied.

'Are you asking if I had something to do with it? Why would you even think that?' Shaun asked.

Suddenly I was ashamed of myself for being so suspicious of Shaun. Matt did seem like the type of person to have a lot of enemies. He most likely slashed my tyres and was a drug addict after all. I was certain that there were probably a lot of people who were out to get him.

'I'm sorry,' I said, 'but I wondered if the two were connected. Please forget I said anything.'

All the way home I kept thinking what a terrible person I was.

'I can't believe you think I had something to do with Matt being bashed up,' Shaun persisted.

This made me feel even worse. I apologised. It was turning out to be a beautiful evening and I wanted to suggest that we go out for dinner on me. We drove in silence only hearing the song 'Total Eclipse of the Heart' which softly came from the radio.

'I can't believe you don't trust me,' Shaun continued to hammer me. 'Do you think I'm a criminal?'

I found myself apologising again and told Shaun that he was not a criminal. When we got out of the car I wrapped my arms around Shaun and embraced him in a giant cuddle. This was not the thing I would generally do but I felt as though I had to do something. Arguing over a person I hardly knew was not the way I envisioned spending my evening. To my delight, Shaun hugged me back and accepted my apology. I found myself feeling bad but happy that Shaun had forgiven me. I decided to bring up my dinner proposal after all but Shaun told me he was tired and wanted to stay home.

We spent the evening having a quiet dinner and in bed, the events of the last couple of hours forgotten. I never found out the truth behind what actually happened with Matt or what the money I had discovered was for. A nice couple with two small children moved into Matt's old place. Matt was never spoken of again. It was like he never existed.

CHAPTER 7
PAST RELATIONSHIPS

My track record with relationships has not been great in the past. In fact, I can quite confidently say that I had not been with anyone that made me happy. They have either wanted to see multiple women or, to put it bluntly, I or they weren't that interested in moving things further.

Firstly, there was Jeremy. I met Jeremy when I was buying a new car. He gave me a business card with his mobile phone number on it. During this time I was going on multiple dates so thought I'd give it a go. We ended up seeing each other close to eighteen months. This was probably a lot longer than it should have gone on for. It seemed I had a habit of doing this. I was never, ever physically attracted to Jeremy and he never mentally stimulated me. This must sound terrible, I know, but it was also true. Intelligence, confidence and a sense of humour are the qualities which were most important to me when it came to choosing a partner. Unfortunately, Jeremy possessed none of these. Looks-wise he wasn't bad and lots of people kept telling me that too. The break-up was horrible and it happened when Jeremy told me he loved me. I unfortunately could not bring myself to say these words as I did not love Jeremy, nor could ever see myself with him in the future. Jeremy wanted marriage and children which I knew was not going to happen with us. Years later, I found out that Jeremy had a nervous breakdown. I didn't ask the person who disclosed this information what happened. It was very disturbing to hear and I was sorry that Jeremy never found the right one for him and wasn't living the happy life he'd dreamed of. If I had heard he'd eventually found happiness, I would have genuinely been happy for him as he truly was a nice guy.

Then there was Geoff. He was my friend Jenny's brother and we met at her birthday party. We spoke a lot that night and I didn't think too much about it until he called me out of the blue. After a long chat I agreed to go out for a coffee with him. Geoff was lovely and we had a great time but I didn't feel like I should take it any further. He gave me a rose on our date which sat in my car wilting for weeks. We swapped a few texts but didn't see each other again until I invited him out with a group of friends hoping to set him up with a friend who was looking for a decent guy. It was during that outing that I realised I could definitely see myself with him. I wasn't sure if the reason for changing my mind was the realisation that he may date my friend or because I didn't give myself a chance to get to know him. We started seeing each other for a few months until he broke my heart. I always suspected that he was seeing other women during this time. In the end, he left me for another woman. I saw this as karma for not giving Geoff a proper chance in the beginning. Who knows what may have happened if I did? I told myself to never dwell on the past. Things happen for a reason and that was obviously not meant to be.

Then there was Edward. He was the one I met who made me forget about Geoff. I was first introduced to Edward at a good friend's fancy dress party. For me it was pretty much lust at first sight. The thing that drew me to him was definitely his cheekiness and confidence rather than his looks. The fact he was dressed as a Private Detective helped too. He wasn't at all a looker. After meeting him, I asked my friend for his number who flatly refused to give it to me claiming he was a player and was seeing multiple women. This upset me as it was up to me to date who I wanted and find these things out for myself. I was extremely determined to see Edward again so ended up stealing his number from my friend's phone. We ended up going on a couple of good dates until the excuses of why he couldn't see me started. After about a year of sporadic emails, texts and mostly cancelled dates we simply grew apart. Looking back, it was a lot of fun while it lasted. Experiences such as these are always the ones you look back on and laugh at.

Shaun and I would sometimes talk about past relationships. This didn't happen very often as soon into our relationship I was quick to learn about Shaun's jealous streak. It was quite severe so I didn't feel like I could be very open about situations, especially as time passed and our relationship grew. Jealousy is a real turn-off for me as I am of the opinion that the past is the past. In the few times I had spoken about my past, Shaun had switched off, which I took as a sign to basically keep my mouth shut. I could tell that Shaun in particular hated when I spoke about Edward which, thinking back, I hardly ever did.

It started one sunny afternoon when Shaun and I were sipping flutes of champagne outside. We both enjoyed doing this when the weather was nice. Sometimes we would talk and other times we would simply sit and read. On this particular occasion we were talking about work until out of nowhere Shaun decided to bring up Edward.

'Edward is such a coward,' Shaun said.

I stared at Shaun in confusion. He didn't even know Edward so how would he know anything about him? Not sure where this was coming from I decided to ask for further details.

'How do you know?' I asked Shaun. 'You haven't even met him.'

'Two of my acquaintances blindfolded him in an alleyway and told him they were going to hold him hostage,' he said. 'He actually pissed his pants before they let him go.' Shaun then collapsed in laughter.

Shaun told me enough to make one thing clear: he

had the power and connections to make things happen. Since the episode with Matt's injury and quick departure, I had no doubt he was not making this up. My heart led me to believe Shaun was innocent in what occurred with Matt but my mind knew better. Nothing he told me, however, suggested that Edward was harmed in any way which was my main concern. It then occurred to me that I would have to watch what I said about people. Shaun was the type of person who was extremely impulsive and obviously did not handle certain situations well. Not understanding why Shaun wanted to bring this up now, I suggested that we talk about something else. If there was anything bad to find out I didn't want to know about it at this particular moment. Shaun wore a look of satisfaction on his face when I said this. I wasn't sure if he was happy because of what he claimed had happened or because he felt that he stood up for me. Either way I was happy we left it at that and decided to take a walk instead.

I was glad for the chance to later perform a Google search on Edward. When scrolling through the search results I discovered that Edward had both a live Facebook and LinkedIn account. I breathed a sigh of relief. Judging by the photos I was able to view on Facebook, it seemed as though Edward was leading a happy and fulfilled life with a young baby in tow. There was a lot I didn't know about Shaun yet. This both excited and frightened me at the same time. It excited me because I was enjoying the relationship as a whole so far, but frightened me because

I didn't know Shaun well enough to know what evil he was capable of. Only time would tell.

CHAPTER 8

NO MORE DRINKS

'D o you want another drink, Carmella?' Cheryl asked me.

I was out with work friends for drinks. We had just finished a work planning session, and what better way to end the day than by having a nice glass of wine. It had been quite a while since I had done this so it was nice to sit back, chill and relax. There were three of us drinking together; myself, Cheryl and Kristen. I hadn't got on that well with either of them when I first started working with them. They both thought that I was after a promotion which was earmarked for Kristen. I have to admit that it probably looked that way as I was trying extremely hard to fit in with the team and particularly with the manager at the time. Once again, being a European in a largely Anglo company, I felt as though I had to make that additional effort to fit in and be accepted. This was the way it had been for most of my life. When the girls got to know me they soon realised that I was only being friendly and wanted to blend in with the team. We had been colleagues and close friends ever since we got that matter sorted.

Tonight they were dying to hear all about Shaun. They had briefly heard about him but there was only so much you could reveal in the work environment. It was nice to be out so I could talk more freely about him. By this stage it had been a few months since I'd moved in with him.

'We want to hear all about what's been happening with Shaun,' Kristen said.

'It's going well so far but it's still early days,' I said.

Sometimes I lay awake at night and thought to myself that maybe I moved in with Shaun too early. Overall the relationship was going well but I still felt I didn't know him as much as I should. There were many things that still played on my mind, particularly the incident which involved Matt and the story of Edward pissing himself in the alleyway. There was nobody I felt I could talk to about these issues, especially with no evidence for either story. We had our differences in some areas but I guessed that came with every relationship. I kept telling myself that I wasn't married to Shaun and there was always a way out if I wanted one. This is what I constantly told myself and it always seemed to console me.

'I hope we get to meet him soon,' said Cheryl.

'Yes, most certainly,' I replied. 'He's picking me up tonight but I'll have to invite him out with us for drinks soon.'

The conversation then shifted to work stuff. Two hours and about four wines later we all felt a bit giddy. As Shaun was picking me up, it was nice to not have to worry about catching public transport home. Being Friday night, there were a lot of people at the bar. Cheryl and Kristen were both single so when a group of men approached us I was happy that it gave them a chance to have a bit of a flirt. There was a lovely guy in the group named Steven who started talking to me. I established straight away that I was in a relationship so it was good to chat with him knowing he had no expectations. I found myself thinking that if I were single I would probably go out with him. Maybe I had these thoughts because it was still early days with Shaun or alternatively that I felt doubtful about the whole situation.

The night came to an abrupt end when I got a text from Shaun advising me that he was parked out the front waiting for me. It was a bit earlier than we had agreed to but I was grateful for the lift. I said goodbye to Steven and told Cheryl and Kristen that Shaun was waiting outside for me. They seemed a little disappointed that I was leaving but walked me out of the bar. The men Cheryl and Kristen were chatting with also followed us out. I spotted Shaun's car and saw him looking out of the window at us. Cheryl and Kristen waved but Shaun continued to stare out the window and didn't acknowledge them which I thought was strange. I hugged Cheryl and Kristen goodbye, telling them that Shaun probably didn't realise that they were my friends who were waving.

I walked to the passenger side of the car, opened the door and got inside. I leaned over and gave Shaun a kiss.

'Hi and thanks so much for picking me up,' I said.

Shaun looked at me for a moment before speaking.

'You smell of alcohol,' he said.

I laughed. 'I did go out for drinks, Shaun,' I replied. 'That's what you do when you go out for drinks, you drink alcohol.'

I found Shaun's remark rather odd but didn't say anything further.

Shaun started the car, kept his eyes on the road and stared straight ahead before speaking again.

'Who were those guys you were outside with?' he asked.

'Oh they were just some guys Cheryl and Kristen met,' I said. 'Why do you ask? Oh and by the way why didn't you wave at the girls?' I pressed on.

'Look Carmella, I'm going to tell you straight,' said Shaun, ignoring my questions. 'I don't like you drinking without me in your company. It's not that I don't trust you but I don't trust the people out there. What if one of those men spiked your drink and I wasn't there to protect you? You could have been raped.'

I took in his words but my first thoughts were that he was being utterly dramatic. Consuming a few wines wouldn't cloud my judgement and I would still be in control of my actions. I was an adult and fully capable of making my own decisions. And being raped? I think I was intelligent enough to know who I should or shouldn't be accepting drinks from. Besides, I enjoyed going out for drinks with my friends and more often than not bought my own drinks. How would I possibly explain to people why I wasn't drinking anything when we went out? Would I have to tell them that my boyfriend wouldn't let me? That would be extremely embarrassing for both myself and, I believed, for Shaun as well.

Shaun continued speaking before I was able to respond to him.

'Please promise me you won't drink anymore, Carmella. This is so important to me,' Shaun said.

He almost begged me which I thought was pathetic. Something inside me told me that this request was totally unreasonable. I had never met someone who had imposed rules on me before and I didn't want to agree to this. I did however feel trapped into saying 'yes' even though I didn't want to. I reluctantly caved in.

'Ok Shaun, if it means that much to you,' I softly said and hated myself as I spoke.

Shaun had a smile on his face for the rest of the drive home. I wasn't sure if this was because he felt that he was protecting me or because he had gotten his way yet again.

Too embarrassed to tell anyone what I'd agreed to, I performed a Google search on this topic to see if anyone else had ever received this type of request from their partner. To my surprise, I found that they had. When reading up on this I found that the majority of opinions stated that this demand was much too controlling. I hoped and prayed to myself that this wasn't the start of something more sinister. Definitely one I had to watch out for.

CHAPTER 9
VIDEO NUDIES

Unlike myself, Shaun found it easy to talk about past relationships as I did not possess a jealous streak. Shaun opened up and told me he was once in a very abusive relationship with a girl named Mila. He met Mila through his best friend when he was eighteen years old. Mila was Dutch, and according to Shaun, looked like a model from France. Tall, blonde with fair skin, she was apparently a real looker. Shaun was crazy about her. He even punched a good friend of his when Mila told Shaun that he had made a move on her.

Shaun and Mila were happy together, inseparable in fact, for a couple of years before their relationship turned sour. The trigger for the change in the relationship was when Mila found out she was unable to have children. At a very early age, Mila's dream was that she always wanted to raise a family. Mila's confidence took a turn for the worse after this and she soon became obsessive over Shaun. Mila accused Shaun of cheating on her when he was dressed up and heading out for job interviews or going out to spend time with his mates when she allowed him.

The physical abuse in their relationship commenced when they attended a movie convention together. Mila supposedly caught Shaun straightening up a cardboard cut-out of Liz Hurley from the movie *Austin Powers: International Man of Mystery* and slapped him in front of a room full of attendees as she thought he had fallen in love with it. Shaun was banned from going to any movie events from that point on.

The slaps and abuse continued over the next six months of their relationship. Mila also found a new way of physically abusing Shaun. She would roughly twist his nose, causing it to bleed heavily and would act like it was a playful game. Being a male, Shaun did not want to tell anybody as he considered this to be a sign of weakness. It was one night at Mila's aunt's house that Shaun had had enough and put a stop to what was happening.

Mila had been niggling Shaun for the entire day. She was jealous of a work colleague who called Shaun earlier that morning wanting advice from a male's perspective about a man she'd been seeing for a year. She suspected he had been cheating on her. Since overhearing this call, Mila had been slapping Shaun and referring to his colleague as his 'new girlfriend'. Things did not improve even after Shaun advised that he did not want to fight and wanted a peaceful night. Mila did not listen nor alter her behaviour. Shaun suddenly snapped when the situation got out of hand when she threw a knife she had used to slice an apple at his face which slashed his right cheek. Shaun grabbed Mila by her hair and threw her across the room yelling floods of abuse at her. Mila's aunt, who also had other guests over that night, kicked Shaun out straight after this incident. It was that night that Shaun and Mila's relationship ended.

It was a Friday night and I was exhausted from work. The time was 6.00 pm and Shaun hadn't arrived home from work yet. I turned on the television and flicked through the channels. The news was on every station which I was not interested in. I hated watching the news as it was always full of bad stories. I then began to look through my massive DVD collection and decided on watching *Suddenly 30* which was an old favourite of mine. I had seen it on numerous occasions and loved all movies with Jennifer Garner in them. I put the DVD in the player and sat down to relax. I was so involved in the movie that I did not hear Shaun come home. I was watching the scene when poor Jenna was out with a man and didn't know what to do when her date stripped down to his boxer shorts. I suddenly heard an angry shout coming from the doorway of the living room.

'YOU ONLY WANTED TO WATCH THAT MOVIE SO YOU CAN SEE THAT MAN NAKED!' Shaun yelled.

The yelling shocked me but not half as much as the

accusation. I could hardly believe my ears that I was actually being yelled at for watching a PG-rated film. Was Shaun really that nuts? I tried to hold back the fury that I was feeling inside. My heart was beating with both fear and rage at the same time and I quickly jumped up from where I had been comfortably seated. I heard myself shouting back.

'Do you know how pathetic you sound right now?' I yelled. 'This is one of my favourite movies and you're accusing me of wanting to watch it because of a man in his boxer shorts?'

Shaun's anger subsided when he saw that I was getting angry.

'Please calm down. I don't want to lose you,' Shaun softly said.

He would certainly lose me if this type of behaviour continued. I wasn't a five-year-old child, I was supposed to be his partner.

'And I don't want to be a clone of Mila as I would hate myself for that,' Shaun continued. 'I want to make our relationship work.'

When I began to protest, he put his finger to my lips.

'I think that it's best that when there is a naked person in a movie that we turn away from the screen,' said Shaun. 'It's the only way to avoid anything like this ever happening again.'

If I was hearing this conversation between two other people I would think they were rehearsing a scene for a movie or play. If it was from a film I was watching,

I would be throwing popcorn at the screen and yelling at the female character to quickly dump that guy. And not wanting to be a clone of Mila? He was Mila's mirror image! I had no idea why I found myself agreeing to this ludicrous suggestion. I wasn't sure who I hated more at that moment, myself or Shaun. The thought of even telling somebody about this situation embarrassed me yet again. I pushed aside the doubts I was feeling and told myself that this wasn't a big deal and something that I could easily do. In reality, I knew I was nuts to have agreed to this. My enjoyment of movies quickly deteriorated as the new rule was put into place. I may as well have donated my entire movie collection to charity as the majority definitely had a scene or two involving nudity. From then on in the relationship, we both quickly turned our heads away from the screen if there was nudity in a movie. This was another controlling behaviour I added to my list.

CHAPTER 10
NEW JOB

To create another focus in my life other than my relationship with Shaun, I decided to look for another career opportunity. This, unlike my relationship, proved to be easy and one actually presented itself to me.

Today was the last working day with my old team at Student Glamour, before I started an extended assignment in another part of the firm. I would definitely miss working with Cheryl, Kristen and the team but it was time for a change. On my last day, I packed my belongings into a cardboard box and moved them to what would be my new place of work, also known as my second home. As the role was still within the same company, I wouldn't be very far from my former colleagues. In fact, I would still be working in the same building but on the next level up.

I met Luke Davenport, who would be my new boss, in the lift one morning. From that day forward we would chat every day about work. Luke was very interested in what I did and mentioned an Event Coordinator position which was available in his team. He was friendly, charismatic and appeared to be someone I could work well with. From what I could tell, the job entailed more money and responsibility and I was after both. After an interview and a glowing reference from my current manager I was successful in securing the position. Luke and I were both rapt. He even bought me a bottle of wine to share with Shaun to celebrate. I was relieved he hadn't offered to take me out for a celebratory drink as trying to say 'no' would've been extremely awkward. This was going to be great!

Walking to work from the train station on my first day, I made a mental list of things I wanted to quickly happen. Introduce myself to the team, organise my desk, initiate weekly one-on-one meetings with Luke and begin to learn about the new tools and systems they used. I was so deep in thought that I didn't realise I had already arrived at my new workplace until I was on the floor.

'You're here early,' said Luke as I took a seat in my new spot.

Luke appeared to be sombre and rather serious today. He was also wearing glasses, which I wasn't aware he wore. They made his face appear sharp. There was also no smile on his usually cheerful face. This was a completely different greeting and vibe from what I was used to getting from Luke. Maybe something bad had happened or there was something on his mind? Either way, I felt that I couldn't ask as I hardly knew him yet.

'Good morning, Luke,' I replied in my usual jovial manner.

Still no smile. Hmm... It was hot and windy outside but the powerful air conditioning was keeping our office cool. Somehow I didn't think that was the only reason for the goose bumps forming on my bare arms. I received a grunt from Luke in return before he stormed off. Enquiring about my induction on his way out didn't seem like the right time to bring it up. I hoped he would be in a better mood by the time he got back.

It was a daily tradition in my former team for us all to get a takeaway coffee from our favourite city cafe during morning tea time. When I received a Skype message from Cheryl asking if I'd like to tag along, I went without even thinking there may be an issue. After a short laugh and gossip with the girls, I returned back to the office with my coffee.

'Where were you?' Luke asked gruffly.

I didn't even notice he was back and nearly dropped my coffee in shock.

'I just grabbed a quick coffee,' I replied.

'That time comes out of your lunch break,' Luke said angrily, pointing a finger at me at the same time.

Whoa! If I'd known that, I wouldn't have gone, I thought to myself. Is having a toilet break deducted from my lunch hour too? Of course I didn't ask this and instead kept quiet.

On a positive note, the team, especially Sheila and Sharon, were absolutely lovely. After lunchtime, we were talking about how gorgeous and hot the weather was outside, but our conversation died down as soon as Luke stormed back to his desk. I wondered if it was always this silent when Luke was around. Shortly after, he raced up to my desk clutching a piece of paper.

'I need a meeting organised with these people in two days from now,' Luke said throwing the piece of paper down on my desk.

I squinted my eyes and looked at the paper, barely able to read his illegible scrawl. There was no explanation on who the attendees were or what the purpose of the meeting was. It was fortunate that with a bit of research on what these people had in common and digging through the system (luckily not much different to the one I was previously working with), that I was able to work it all out. With a bit of luck Luke would realise what a gun I was and that I could be relied on to complete any task. This might be my opportunity to shine. I was bargaining on this to improve my already shaky working relationship with Luke. Why he behaved like this towards me, I wasn't sure. I would've thought he would be happy to have me in his team.

Today was meeting day and I was both nervous and excited at the same time. The meeting entailed a group of stakeholders getting together to discuss an upcoming fundraiser for student scholarships. I managed to book the largest meeting room in the building as well as organise a selection of delicious finger foods for lunch. There was a lot of chatter around the room and some great ideas for the forthcoming event. I was sure to make copious notes in order to capture all their suggestions. Smiling as I was working, I was very comfortable and in my element being the prime organiser of this meeting. During the lunch break, I sat with Leanne and Christine, two women I used to work with, who also worked in this building. Engrossed in conversation, I took a quick glance at Luke who had a half-smile plastered on his face. With his recent attitude I couldn't even begin to tell if that meant he was happy or not. I just assumed he was pleased as that was the closest thing to a smile I had seen on his face since I commenced working with him.

The lunch break was soon over and everyone took a seat for the afternoon PowerPoint session. I had managed to organise for a man named Michael Newton from a neighbouring event management company to talk about a similar event they had run. Perfectly attired in an impeccably pressed white shirt, blue blazer and slacks, Michael took the stand in front of the room. Many of the people in the room were very excited to hear from Michael. They mentioned this to me via email when I sent the papers for the meeting through to them. I handed out a copy of the presentation to everyone. When I reached Luke, he appeared incandescent with rage. I decided to ignore this for the moment. As far as I could tell, the day was so far excelling. Once Michael's talk had finished, the room broke out into a round of applause. That concluded the day.

As people departed from the meeting they congratulated me on a job well done and told me how nice it was to meet me. I was left feeling on a high. The meeting room was left in quite a state of disarray so I went about disposing cups, plates, and recycling paper. Singing to myself while cleaning, I didn't notice that Luke had walked back into the room until he tapped me on the shoulder. I turned around. Make an effort Carmella, I told myself.

'What did you think of today?' I asked brightly. 'Everyone seemed to enjoy it.'

I was very pleased with myself and knew that meeting was one hundred per cent perfect.

'Don't you ever do that again,' Luke replied.

He looked like an evil monster. I wanted to be sarcastic and reply, 'Don't do what? Host a successful meeting?' Instead I chose to listen to Luke's next words. He was holding up a hard copy of Michael's PowerPoint presentation. I unfortunately had no idea what he meant and he must have been able to tell by the blank look on my face.

'THE STAPLE!' Luke screamed at me. 'Next time, hole punch these and place them in folders.'

I was too shocked to even respond as Luke stormed out the door. He wanted to make a scene for the sake of a staple? Like that could've made a difference to the success of the meeting! I thought he may have at least thanked me for how today went, but no such luck. Today's success was meant to show Luke how capable I was of delivering but he obviously had other ideas. I couldn't help the tears which started to form in my eyes. They were not only caused by how hurt I was feeling but also by anger. I had a very bad feeling about this job. It certainly was not going to be easy.

CHAPTER 11
MEETING SHAUN'S FAMILY

One of the odd features of Shaun's and my relationship was that I hadn't met his family despite being together for some time. I remarked about this to him frequently. So it came as a big surprise to me to suddenly get an invitation to meet his family at no notice. Not only were his parents going to be there but also his sister, her children and Shaun's grandmother.

It all started shortly after I arrived home from work one day when Kristen came over for a visit. I hugged her as she walked in the door. With her she had brought the latest novel by Stephen King. What a gem! Reading books rather than watching movies was definitely the safest option for me nowadays. I did sometimes however wonder if Shaun would take note of what I was reading and research my books to see if they contained written scenes of nudity. That bridge would be crossed if it ever came to that.

Shaun had called and texted me six times in the fifteen minutes that Kristen hung around for. Kristen gave me an odd look before she questioned Shaun's 'obsessive' behaviour as she called it. I laughed at Kristen's words. After a failed number of relationships Kristen was still looking for her 'Mr Right'. Kristen was one of those women who believed that there was only one right person for everyone out there. We had had numerous heated discussions on this issue as our opinions could not be more different on this topic. I was, at that stage, content in my relationship with Shaun (minus the no drinking and no watching nudity in movies rules) but if it didn't work out I could also be happy with someone else. This I would never in one million years tell him, though.

I paused and thought about Kristen's comment. Kristen knew nothing of the rules being imposed on me and her opinion was already negative. She had never even met Shaun apart from the time he hadn't waved at her and Cheryl when he picked me up from drinks that one time. It wasn't exactly a great introduction. Should I be concerned or was she (like Sarah) perhaps a bit jealous? Before I had time to debate with myself, my phone binged again with another text from Shaun. This time it was to inform me that we were going to his family's house for dinner that evening. Wow, I thought to myself, thanks heaps for the warning. Saying a quick goodbye to Kristen,

I went to examine my closet. I didn't know the first thing to wear to what could be my future in-laws' place.

I wasn't prepared for what I saw when we drove up to Shaun's parents' place. It was a beautiful mansion right next to the beach. This was something Shaun failed to mention to me. I felt a bit underdressed in my faded denim jeans and light pink jumper. It was too late to worry about any of that now. With a huge smile plastered across my face I got out of the car. We arrived at the front door, a Celtic cross right in the centre of it. I was sincerely going to try and make the most out of this.

We walked into Shaun's parents' place and the first thing I noticed was all the beautiful food that had been prepared. I wondered if this was their normal dinner or if they made a special effort for me? I would have been flattered if it were the latter. Laid out on their long dining room table was a roast chicken, a variety of roasted vegetables, salads and three different pasta dishes. There was also a separate table with a selection of different desserts. Shaun's mother, Shauna, who I'd never met but instantly recognised from the photos Shaun had on display, gave me a half-smile before she grabbed my hand and showed me to a seat at the table.

'I hope you will find something you like to eat,' Shauna said to me. 'I wasn't sure what Wogs like to eat.'

Whoa, that really stung! That remark was like a slap in the face. I hadn't been referred to as a Wog in years. So that at least explained the effort with the food. On a positive note, Shaun had at least warned them that I was Italian, I guess. That showed me he wasn't ashamed of me in front of his family. Let it slide, Carmella, I told myself. To my surprise Shaun laughed. This was definitely a shift in attitude from our first date in the clothes store.

'She didn't mean it the way it sounded,' Shaun said to me. 'My mum doesn't know how to express herself. Look at the trouble she has gone to in preparing dinner for you.'

Hmm, so it seemed Shaun might be a bit of a mama's boy. I reserved my judgement for the moment.

Right then his niece and nephew ran across the kitchen, jumped on Shaun and nearly toppled him over. All curly-haired, blonde and blue-eyed, they were extremely cute. I recognised his niece, Beatrice, as she attended the same school in grade prep with Emilio who was my nephew.

'Come on, Uncle Shaun,' said James. 'Let's go and play Street Fighter.'

I watched as he played with them, commentating throughout the entire game. He clearly let them beat him which had them in fits of giggles as they referred to him as hopeless. It was cute to watch.

'Hey James, let Carmella play you,' Shaun said. 'She's really good and might beat you.'

James turned and stared at me. He scrunched his eyes which made their beautiful blue colour appear icy and cruel.

'No way! She's ugly,' replied James.

James suddenly reminded me of a nasty kid I went to primary school with. He always teased me and referred to me as a Wog. I directed my steely dark eyes right back at James.

'I don't want to play with you anyway,' I replied. 'I'd

beat you and you'd cry.'

My reply to James might've made me sound immature but it felt good to stand up for myself. Shaun's eyes shifted in James' direction and then mine. He then shrugged his shoulders and continued to play. I started to feel very awkward and uncomfortable at this gathering. It felt as though nobody liked or wanted me there and that included Shaun.

At dinner, Anita, who was Shaun's sister, asked me about my work. I happily talked about my experience and expertise in event management and how much I loved my job. Shaun's father hadn't said a word since I walked into the house. I got the impression that he was maybe a little reserved. Nobody seemed at all engaged or interested with what I was saying. At that moment Shauna turned to me and smiled. Excellent, I thought, someone was finally going to ask me a question.

'Do you have one of those jobs that only disadvantaged people can get?' Shauna asked.

At that moment I just wanted to crawl under the table and hide. How much more of this could I take? It was as though they had never seen or met a person who was Italian before.

Once Shaun's sister and children left, Shaun and I both sat outside in the backyard with Shaun's parents and grandmother. I didn't say much, nor did anyone else. I simply enjoyed the peace.

The night then finally came to an end and we said goodbye. I turned to wave when I reached the car door right in time to see Shaun's grandmother spit disgustedly while looking straight in my direction. I was feeling angry but also relieved that the night was finally over.

In the car on the way home Shaun told me how much fun he had.

'The family really took to you, Carmella,' Shaun said.

We must've been present at different gatherings. I half-smiled at Shaun but didn't say anything. Shaun was either blind or in denial about the way I was treated by his family.

That night lying in bed I figured something out. Shaun was one of those men who thought that his family could do no wrong. Is that something I could live with? I'd say I could short-term, but for the rest of my life? I vowed to myself that if that ever happened again I would stand up for myself. There was no point in these issues being raised with Shaun. I reminded myself that Shaun had a lot of positive attributes. He was intelligent, attractive, charming and very likeable. Besides, for the first time I liked being with someone who paid me a lot of attention and I got a lot of that from him. He loved me and had told me so on many occasions and I must admit that was something I so craved during this time of my life. I decided to let the events of this evening slide. Shaun's family's feelings about our relationship could possibly change as time went on. Things could only improve, right?

CHAPTER 12
WEEKEND AWAY

I was ecstatic when Shaun suggested a weekend away. I suspected Shaun secretly knew that I was feeling a bit disheartened after dinner with his family. The plan was to go to Daylesford and stay in a bed and breakfast. I was a little disappointed when at the last minute there was a change of plan. Instead of the little cottage Shaun was supposed to book, we would be staying in a caravan instead. I decided to lighten up as I was still excited about our first weekend getaway together as a couple. This was going to be fun.

As we sped down the highway with the music blaring, I found myself thrilled to be going somewhere. There weren't many cars around so it was like we owned this part of the world. Once we got closer to what would be our home for the next couple of days, we stopped the car and took a walk. There were lovely cafes and cute little trinket stores everywhere. I welcomed the opportunity to stop for a few purchases before we jumped in the car again and drove on.

The caravan was as I expected, rundown and shabby. Shaun must've noticed my face drop a little as it didn't take him long to try and lift my spirits.

'I have some amazing plans for us tonight, babe,' Shaun said. 'I've made reservations at a beautiful Italian restaurant and then I thought we could stay in and share a bottle of wine together.'

I smiled. At least we weren't going to stay in the caravan the entire time. Besides, it was all about the company. The caravan would only be somewhere to go back to at the end of the night.

The restaurant was bustling when we got there but I loved the atmosphere. It was good that Shaun made a reservation as there was no way we would've been seen to otherwise. We ordered garlic bread to start with, followed by some pasta dishes. The food looked delicious based on the presentation of the meals other diners around us had. Shaun took my hand from across the table as we both drank our wine.

'I'm so glad we did this,' Shaun said. 'I love spending time alone with you and having you to myself.'

My heart fluttered inside my chest. I had mixed emotions. A part of me was happy Shaun felt this way but then the other part of me thought about the incidents which had occurred throughout our relationship.

The waiter then brought our garlic bread over to us. It looked divine with crispy outside edges and the inside covered with melted garlic and herb butter. Shaun and I continued talking as I grabbed a piece from the plate and took a bite. Like most times when I eat, a piece of food got stuck on my tooth. I didn't want to interrupt Shaun's chatter so I slid my tongue over my top back tooth and successfully managed to get it off. Like the flick of a light switch, Shaun's mood instantly changed.

'I need to get out of here,' Shaun said. 'I'm suddenly not feeling so well.'

I wondered what had happened. We were having such a pleasant evening. This was so sudden.

'Shaun, are you OK?' I asked.

Before he could even reply, Shaun was halfway to the entrance of the restaurant, leaving me with the bill.

The short car ride back to the caravan park was extremely quiet. I made a decision not to say anything until we were safely ensconced in the caravan. Once we had parked the car, Shaun hurriedly got out and headed into the caravan and I followed closely behind. Instantly I realised that, rather than being sick, Shaun was in fact angry about something.

'I saw you winking at that guy, Carmella,' Shaun said. 'The one sitting at the table in front of us.'

What table? Which guy? I asked myself these questions. This wasn't the first time something like this had happened. I found myself thinking back to the incident with Alan when I first moved in with Shaun. I was getting a little tired of all these accusations. If I was such a bad person why didn't he simply call the relationship off?

'It was when you were eating the garlic bread,' Shaun continued.

I found myself giggling as Shaun said this. It must've been when I was trying to remove the food from my tooth. I explained this to Shaun.

'I had a piece of garlic bread on my tooth, Shaun,' I said. 'My eye sometimes closes when I use my tongue to try and get it out.'

Shaun didn't appear to be listening and was pacing around the caravan frantically.

'I did all of this for you, Carmella,' said Shaun. 'And all you can think of is looking at other men.'

I suddenly felt ashamed as Shaun said these words. He was doing everything he could to make this weekend special and I started to feel ungrateful. I did however remind myself that I did not wink at some random man sitting at a nearby table at the restaurant. Trying to calm Shaun down, I suggested he take a few moments for himself.

'Listen, Shaun, I don't know what you think happened but I didn't do anything,' I said. 'Go freshen up while I open up that bottle of wine you so generously bought for us.'

Shaun took a little walk leaving me alone with my thoughts. On his return his mood was so bright that I thought he was a different person. I handed him one of the glasses I poured, determined to not have this weekend ruined. We took a seat on the worn-out lounge. After a few sips of wine I noticed that Shaun seemed to be drowsy and his eyes began to droop.

'Are you tired?' I asked Shaun. 'We can go to sleep if you like.'

His next words of confession made my blood freeze.

'I've just swallowed a handful of sleeping pills,' Shaun announced. He almost sounded proud of this like it was some sort of accomplishment. 'I do regret it now though.'

A handful of sleeping pills? Was he insane? I totally pass out on taking just one. Grabbing Shaun's arm, I raced him to the bathroom and watched as he heaved out the contents of his stomach. I was relieved that this seemed to have worked and that after a few moments Shaun was feeling better and we were seated back on the lounge. I put my face in both hands.

'Why, Shaun?' I asked. 'Why would you do that?'

I felt so drained as I asked Shaun these questions.

'I thought you didn't want to be with me,' said Shaun.

'Let's go to bed and talk in the morning,' I suggested.

We both got into bed. The bed smelled of dust and mould but I tried to push that aside. I didn't think either of us felt like talking at that particular moment.

When we both woke up the next day, Shaun announced that he wanted to go home.

'This place is bad luck,' Shaun said to me. 'Let's go home.'

I agreed and didn't feel like staying in a place where Shaun may have had the intention of taking his own life. Was it my fault? Should I feel guilty? At that moment I didn't feel I could share what had happened with anyone. I felt very empty and alone.

On the way out Shaun punched a statue of a rooster that had been sitting on top of the small television.

'I hate this fucking rooster,' Shaun said. 'It has been staring at me since I got here.'

The statue smashed onto the ground and shattered into tiny pieces. The rooster had actually been quite cute. Shaun's paranoid feelings came to the surface right then and there if he thought a statue had been staring at him. I didn't argue as my main focus was to get away from the caravan and this weekend away.

On the way out, I offered to go and hand the caravan keys back to reception. I told the receptionist who wore a name tag that read 'Norman' that we were leaving early due to a family emergency. Slipping him a twenty dollar bill I also let him know that we accidentally broke the rooster statue. Thanking me, he told me to come back again soon. I smiled and told him to have a nice day, thinking I could not get away from there quick enough.

CHAPTER 13
MANIAC BEHAVIOUR

One evening after work I had planned a coffee date with Sarah. I hadn't been out with her since I'd moved out to live with Shaun and I really missed her. She was eager to speak to me about a new guy she had just met and I couldn't wait to hear all about it. It took me a lot of courage to tell Shaun about my meeting with Sarah, to which he had no response. I was becoming less comfortable in communicating things to Shaun. Getting out and being social with other people was something I desperately needed. Too much had been going on with Shaun lately and I needed an escape from it all. I was hoping he would wish me a good time but I got none of that.

I was excited to catch up with Sarah and to be in her company. I gave her a giant hug when I met her. She hugged me back, most likely unaware of how happy I was to be there. Just seeing her brought back memories of all the good times we'd shared when we lived together. My life was mine back then and I felt like it was becoming less so lately.

The night was gloriously mild so we decided to sit at an outside table. Once seated, her friendly chatter and warm presence made me feel relaxed. The guy she had met, named Sam, seemed like an absolute dream. They met online and had already been on about half a dozen dates. Sam was a lawyer and undertook a lot of travel which Sarah would've loved. Sarah worked in a travel agency so I could very well imagine all the deals she had promised Sam. The fact that I had not heard about any of this made me realise that it had been so long since I had spoken with her. It also made me feel slightly jealous but that didn't last when I could see how happy she was. Sarah's mood was infectious and I couldn't help the smile which was constantly on my face. We were so engaged in conversation that we did not notice the waiter come up to us. He asked us if there was anything he could get for us. Sarah ordered a wine which at that moment I would've killed for. The waiter also rattled off a lot of drink specials including various cocktails which sounded delightful. I ended up ordering an iced coffee. Clearly not impressed with my decision not to have an alcoholic beverage, Sarah began to protest loudly.

'Come on, Carmella!' Sarah said. 'Don't tell me you don't want a drink? You never refuse one, and besides it has been ages since I've seen you.'

Sarah had a point but didn't know of Shaun's pathetic rule which was imposed on me. I remembered my promise about not drinking alcohol without his presence and asked myself if he would ever find out. I then decided, what the heck. His reason for me not consuming alcohol without him was that he didn't trust others around me. I decided to have one, convincing myself that I was in Sarah's company who would look after me if anything did go wrong. I heard myself quickly changing my order and telling the waiter that I wanted a flute of pink champagne instead. The words were out of my mouth before I even made a firm decision. Sarah and I continued to talk until our drinks arrived. That first sip of my alcoholic beverage never tasted so good. Could it be because I had control of the situation and was defying Shaun? Yes, I found that I thoroughly enjoyed that I had disobeyed him. It wasn't that I wanted to be bad, but because I didn't agree with what was put upon me. In that moment I did not at all regret the decision.

Not long after, when Sarah and I were relaxing over our drinks, we heard the sound of a car furiously driving up and down the street.

'What a maniac,' Sarah said. 'Does he realise that he can kill someone with that dangerous behaviour?'

I glanced towards the street and saw that it was Shaun's car. This was not Shaun's first act of craziness but this I believed had reached a new level of madness. He was actually checking up on me as I had informed him where I would be meeting Sarah. This reminded me of a scene in a thriller movie about obsession but instead it was reality. Our eyes locked when he drove past and I clearly saw the anger on his face. I also noticed that his eyes had diverted to the champagne flute in front of me. I found myself suddenly filled with anxiety and my hands became fidgety under the table. Why had I ever agreed to this rule? It was so unfair and unjust. Sarah noticed the rapid change in my behaviour and asked if I was OK. I told her I had developed a headache and excused myself to go to the toilet. Thank goodness she had not recognised his car.

Once in there, I sat inside a cubicle and tried to steady my breathing. It was then that I heard my phone and its non-stop beeping. I pulled the phone out of my bag and saw a bombardment of text messages from the deranged Shaun.

```
Nice coffee or should I say champagne?
Sarah is a slut.
I'll be waiting for you in the park across the road.
You better be out in ten minutes before I come
there myself and get you.
```

I couldn't fight back the tears of frustration and anger that ran down my face. I was so scared and upset by the entire situation. I had no choice but to clean my face and walk back out to Sarah.

Sarah smiled when I returned, but she could see that I was upset. I told her my headache was getting worse and that I'd better go before I found it difficult to get home.

Sarah was disappointed but understood. She also offered to drive me home but I told her that I would be OK. I also said that we would do it again soon, fully aware that I would not be able to fulfil this promise.

Sarah and I walked to her car parked just outside the bar and I watched her drive off. I stood there watching for as long as I could, at the same time ensuring that I wouldn't be later than ten minutes getting to the park where a very crazy and unstable man would be waiting for me.

I arrived at the car. Shaun had the window down and was staring out at me. His usually flat, neat hair was now pushed up into the shape of two devil horns. I thought his ridiculous new hairstyle was a tactic to scare me and keep me in his control. He looked bizarre and like a freak at the same time.

'Get in,' he said when I was standing by the car window near the driver's seat.

'I told you I would catch a train home,' I said calmly.

The look Shaun gave me made me get in the car, but only reluctantly. There were lots of people around and the last thing I felt like doing was causing a scene. Anything could happen with the mood Shaun appeared to be in. As we drove away, I told Shaun how uncomfortable I was that he had followed me.

'You say you love me but with that comes trust,' I told him.

I knew I had put my foot in it with that comment. Shaun had caught me drinking even though I promised that I wouldn't. There I was talking about trust! Shaun however didn't bite and was unusually quiet as he kept driving.

Once we were at home, Shaun pulled out a bottle of scotch and told me that if I could drink with my friends then I could drink with him. Before I could protest and say that I didn't like scotch, he pulled out two glasses and filled them. I felt I had no choice but to drink it. The burning sensation it gave me made me sick but I finished the glass. Shaun filled my glass again so I kept drinking. I felt like this was a drinking contest but one I had no control over and didn't want to participate in. I wasn't sure how long this went on for, but the next thing I realised was that I was being carried into our bedroom and onto the bed. Shaun roughly took my clothes off and pulled his pants down. His hands cupped my breasts which both excited me and hurt at the same time. Before I knew it, Shaun got on top of me which gave me mixed emotions. There was a part of me which couldn't stand what he had done to me tonight. Yet, there was also a strange feeling from within that wanted nothing more than to have sex with him. I went along with Shaun's sexual ideas and blamed the alcohol. My body's response also let me down and I really hated myself for that. The last words I heard before I totally passed out were, 'Don't you ever disobey me again.'

CHAPTER 14
MORNING TWEETS
AND A VICIOUS BOSS

The next day was Thursday. I woke up with Shaun lying beside me. I didn't remember much of what happened last night and wasn't sure if it was worth the effort of trying to recollect the specifics of it. Something told me that it was probably best to put it behind me because if I remembered, I wouldn't like it. Shaun stirred beside me and it seemed as though he was dreaming. He did a lot of that. Whenever I asked him what his dreams were about, his expression turned dark and deadly and I got no response. Maybe it was a good idea not to ask about that either. Shaun's breathing eventually steadied, which told me that he was falling back asleep.

I had a big day in the office today, preparing for an event which our team would host tomorrow. There would be no time for resting at work so lying in bed for a few more moments today seemed logical. It was a beautiful spring morning and the chirping of the birds seemed so peaceful and reassuring to me. The steady, comforting rhythm of their tweeting put me back into a peaceful sleep. This did not last. I was quickly jolted awake by Shaun's outrageous yelling.

'SHUT UP!' he screamed.

Just to clarify, his words were directed at the birds and not me. The beautiful singing of the birds of course continued. I got out of bed, sighed and prepared to get ready for work. Shaun continued to mutter obscenities under his breath while trying to get back to sleep. I found this quite amusing and chuckled to myself, enjoying the harmonious twittering of the birds even more. Leaving one loony at home, it was time to go and face the other one who awaited me at work. What was with the species of men in my life lately?

Once upon a time I used to love work. I loved the busyness, wearing new clothes and putting on make-up. The whole vibe of work used to make me feel so good. Since accepting this new role it felt as though I was heading to a funeral each morning. I truly thought things would work with Luke but the days seemed to be getting worse and worse. Luke supposedly hired me simply because I was eminently qualified and hungry for this type of work. It seemed to me that what Luke really wanted was a punching bag as that was what I was being used for. Since the whole 'I don't like staples' episode, I had tried different tactics by clarifying with Luke exactly what he was after, rather than being proactive. This still didn't work, so I was at a loss figuring out what success would look like to Luke.

The team was in event-preparation mode when I walked into work that morning. Luke arrived fashionably late after ordering the rest of the team to be in early.

'Carmella, get onto the name tags now,' said Luke. 'There are an additional one hundred people attending that we didn't know about.'

I was livid. Firstly, where did Luke get off barking orders at me regarding basic admin tasks? The coordination of this event was my job to sort out. Secondly, one hundred people was a fair few late guests. Nonetheless, I politely smiled, furiously working out what additional duties I needed to tackle for this event to be a success. Clearly, Luke wanted the event to be a failure on my part. Why he wanted this, I didn't know, as this would more than likely reflect poorly on his management and competence.

That day, and into the evening, the team was working their butts off. The venue which we visited earlier that day looked spectacular. After some tough negotiation with the venue we finally figured out a way to accommodate all the last minute guests. I was certain Luke knew about these guests long ago but of course failed to tell me. Jobs listed on the checklist were all completed. Surely this would make Luke happy. I didn't like my chances though. It was 7.30 pm by the time everything was done.

'Luke, everything is set for tomorrow,' I exclaimed happily. 'I'm going home.'

As expected Luke's only response was to scowl which

I was very familiar with by now. I'd worked out that the silent treatment was his way of trying to make people feel guilty so that they would stay at work longer. I wouldn't buy into that as it was late enough. I noticed that Sheila was still at work. Sheila was probably one of the nicest people I'd met, although very quiet. I always felt calmer in her soothing presence. Sheila had a wealth of knowledge and experience and I really couldn't understand why someone like her wanted to work with Luke.

'Why aren't you going home?' I asked Sheila.

'I still have a few things left to do,' Sheila replied quietly.

Odd, I thought to myself. I was more than sure I heard her tell someone earlier that week that she was going through a quiet period at work. Working on this major event hadn't been a part of her role.

The next morning, as predicted, my nerves and anxiety were worse than I had experienced in a long time. Morning tweeting sounded once again and the sound was calming until Shaun yelled at the birds to shut up. This time however he threatened to shoot them with his friend's shotgun. Did he actually believe the birds would be scared of this threat and keep quiet? Rolling my eyes, I quickly got ready and raced out the door to go to work.

I was proud that my great attention to detail in every task associated with the event made it a huge success. Luke's final attempt at trying to sabotage me and catch me off guard did not work. His list of attendees did not include Carla who was the head of our company. My first thought was that Luke of course did that on purpose. Luke was not at all prepared by Carla's fond embrace when she saw me. Carla, a beautiful and elegant woman in her mid-fifties was the person who initially hired me.

'It's so lovely to see you again,' Carla said to me. 'I didn't realise you and Luke were now working together. What a dream team!'

Ha! Little did she know. Carla was not at all fussed about not having a name tag and in fact wore her own stylish and sophisticated, personalised one.

When the event ended, the team went back to the office for celebratory drinks. I of course only sipped on a tepid mineral water as that was all I was allowed to have. Luke as expected made no positive comments regarding the day; he claimed that Carla not having a name badge had been the worst thing to happen to him in his entire professional career.

After drinks, Sharon and I walked to the train station together. Sheila declined our offer when we asked her to walk with us to the train station, deciding to work back instead. What was with her lately? Leaving Luke behind at work was always the best part of my day. I didn't give it a further thought as I was so pleased with myself. Luke was not invincible and I had been victorious. I did know this meant that I would have to keep an even closer watch over what his next move would be.

CHAPTER 15
FACEBOOK THREAT

Facebook had been a big part of my life since I'd stopped seeing my friends. It was the only form of communication I had left with the ones who still spoke to me. Since my night out with Sarah, I had not seen anybody. It was nice to see the pictures my friends posted of their nights out drinking and to keep in the know with what was happening and who was seeing who. It gave me a sense of security in holding on to the life I used to have. My friends had no idea what kind of domineering man I was involved with. Every time a friend of mine wanted to catch up I'd blame it on work and explained I had no time. They either seemed to accept that or were too busy with their own lives to notice what was going on.

The phone call came out of the blue one day when I was at work. I walked back to my desk holding a strong cup of coffee, hoping it would get me through my work day. As I sat down, I heard Luke slam down the phone and yell, 'Take a long walk off a short pier!' I sighed and knew that this was going to be a long day. Luke became more and more impossible to work with as the days went on. Not long after I sat down, the phone on my desk began to ring. I picked up the phone, said hello and was surprised to hear my friend, Paul, on the other end of the line. Paul and I worked together years ago at Kmart during our high school years and instantly became great friends. There was never anything between us and we unfortunately lost contact after Paul moved interstate a couple of years ago to explore further career opportunities.

'Hi, Carmella,' Paul said hesitantly.

'Oh hey, Paul! How are you?' I replied as I recognised his voice straight away. 'What a lovely surprise to hear from you. How have you been? How is Sydney?'

I heard Luke grunt from behind me and took that as a sign to keep the conversation short.

'Yeah, good … ummm … I hate to ring you at work with this but your boyfriend threatened to get me,' Paul replied. 'I didn't feel safe texting or calling you out of work hours in case he had your phone.'

As Paul said these words, my heart began to pound and I felt like I was going to faint. Shaun threatened to get Paul? Surely Paul must have this wrong, I thought. Shaun didn't know Paul and I certainly hadn't mentioned him.

'Threatened you? What do you mean?' I asked.

'He emailed me in response to a group Facebook

message I sent about changing my email address,' Paul explained. 'You had better be careful, Carmella, as he's obviously tracking your Facebook account.'

I asked Paul to forward me a copy of the message before we said goodbye. It was such a terrible shame to hear from Paul under these circumstances. I was absolutely horrified as I read the words Shaun had creatively put together and sent to Paul.

'Listen Pauly, don't you ever contact my woman or I'll get you. Got it boy? This is not a threat but a promise. I will literally break you. I KNOW WHERE YOU ARE AT ALL TIMES. I have people watching you. Leave Carmella alone you weak bi★&h.

Nothing prepared me for what I read. The language and tone of the words in this disgraceful email made me feel sick to the stomach as this was coming from the person I was seeing and shared a bed with.

I didn't know what was worse for me that evening; staying at work or going home. For that day, I would have to say going home was probably worse. Saying goodnight to the rest of my colleagues I realised it was time for me to leave work, head home and see what awaited me.

As I walked slowly to the train station, I thought about how I would approach the situation. There was no way I could simply ignore this. If he had threatened one of my male friends, he could surely do it again.

Shaun was sitting down watching TV when I walked into the house that night.

'You look nice today,' Shaun said, smiling when he saw me.

I looked down at my old black trouser suit I had worn many times and walked into the kitchen to get myself a drink. He must've realised there was a strong chance I would know what happened with Paul by this stage.

'I got an interesting phone call today,' I said as I approached the lounge room.

'Oh, do tell. I need something to make my day exciting,' Shaun replied. 'I've been dealing with annoying customers all day.'

'My friend, Paul, called me today,' I continued. 'He forwarded me an email that you sent him, threatening to get him. He was my friend who used to work with me when we were teenagers. How could you do that? And how did you get his details? Have you been snooping through my Facebook account?'

Shaun laughed, ushering me to take a seat on the couch next to him.

'I was only joking. Come on, Carmella!' Shaun said. 'I had one too many drinks last night. I would never spy on you. You left your account open and I happened to see it.'

I found myself thinking that thank goodness this was the only email I had from a male sitting in my Facebook messenger account. Who knows what else Shaun could've done if there was anything from anyone else?

'Nothing has ever happened between us,' I said softly.

Shaun suddenly turned angry.

'I never once suspected that,' he said. 'I can't begin to imagine many men being interested in you before me. You're not exactly supermodel material.'

His words stung me. What bothered me the most was that he knew exactly how to get under my skin. Being overweight when young greatly impacted on my confidence when growing up. I hadn't thought about my past weight issues for a little while now and feelings of self-doubt started to overwhelm me.

Shaun angrily threw down the TV remote control and stormed out of the room.

'I don't even know why we're having this conversation to begin with,' Shaun spat. 'If this guy is so important maybe you should go and be with him.'

I started to panic. I was afraid that if Shaun left me, I would not be able to find anybody else. My greatest fear was being alone. These feelings always presented themselves when I became self-conscious about my weight even though I had very strong doubts about my relationship with Shaun. I hurried after Shaun and apologised even though I knew I wasn't wrong. He told me he loved me and didn't want anyone or anything getting in the way of our relationship. Shaun then asked me to do something very important for him. I wondered what it would be this time. My life was already being stripped from me. I wasn't sure if I could handle much more being taken from me. I didn't have to wait long to find out. Shaun advised that it would be a good idea for both of us to close down our Facebook accounts. He went on to further explain his reasons for this, being that nobody of the opposite sex would be able to contact us through this medium and we would both therefore avoid situations of jealousy. I was far from jealous of any friendships Shaun had with females but found myself, with a heavy heart, agreeing to this request. This was such an important element in my life, keeping in touch with the outside world. Shaun and I both watched one another as we deactivated our accounts. We then had sex and Shaun held me close afterwards. I knew this relationship was wrong and I felt a sense of entrapment.

I needed a way out.

CHAPTER 16

THE TRUSTY AMEERA

After a number of urgings from my trusted General Practitioner, Patricia, I finally took her advice to see a psychologist. Her words which reinforced my decision to do so were, 'I do not want you here when you are forty years old complaining about the same issues.' I had told Patricia a little of what was going on but not the entire story which included some of the things I was banned from doing. She had given me a referral for a woman in the city who came highly recommended. This was convenient for me as I could either go before or after work. This situation remained in my control and not Shaun's. I was happy about that.

I was extremely nervous before my first appointment as I had never been to a psychologist before. I could recall one of my friends telling me that for her it was a great experience. She got to chat for an entire hour without interruption which suited her perfectly. Being more of an introvert, I wasn't sure that I would feel the same way. The suit I put on for work that morning was one of my more formal ones. I felt that if I looked professional, my situation would be taken more seriously. There was a lot I had to tell and even I had to admit that some of my examples sounded pathetic. The situation sounded pretty black and white, that I should up and go. Unfortunately it wasn't that easy. The appointment I made was an after work one. I took the opportunity to sneak out of the office when Luke was at a meeting. There was no way I would want Luke or anybody else in the office knowing about my appointment.

My first impression of Dr Ameera Hassan was that she was reserved without being a snob. Slim with petite features, she had a presence about her which seemed to calm me. She also had an air of confidence about her which I guess came from being highly educated. After being given the referral, I did some research on her. Ameera was both a psychologist and a lawyer.

I entered her office which was clean, neat and cosy. She took a seat and I sat down in the chair directly in front of her. It was silent for a few moments before Ameera introduced herself with a soft smile. I explained that I had never been to a psychologist before so didn't know what to expect. Ameera explained that the first session would be a 'getting to know you' one. We spent the next hour talking about what work I do, my hobbies and my family. I was freely able to talk about all of this but froze when it came to talking about my grandparents on my mother's side. The only grandparent I ever grew up with was my mother's stepfather. Our family spent a lot of time with him when my grandmother died. Grandparents are supposed to be like second parents to their grandchildren such as giving them sweets, providing comfort when they're upset and taking them out to places like the movies or the zoo. The only memories I had were being told off when reading too loudly or being told not to go into the cupboard for snacks when visiting. I always felt a bit ripped off when I heard stories from other people about growing up with grandparents and often wondered what my mother's real father was like. Close relationships with grandparents was something I hoped to ensure for my children when or if I had them. Here was yet another example of a negative male role model in my life.

'I would prefer it if we stop talking about my step-grandfather,' I said.

Ameera accepted this and we moved on. I explained that the reason I made the decision to see a psychologist was to talk about my current relationship.

'We will focus on that in the next session,' Ameera advised.

I paid for my session and made my way out the door. Ameera sent me home with some breathing exercises to practice in times of stress and anxiety. I was feeling cynical about this but decided to give them a go if I felt the need to. I felt positive after the session as I saw it as a step to making my life a happy one again.

'You're home late,' Shaun said when I walked in through the front door.

'Late night in the office, you know the way this job is,' I replied.

'So how was the therapy session?' Shaun asked.

I slowly put my bag down on the bench and turned to face Shaun who was twirling my appointment card in his hand. He was looking at me with a wicked smile on his face.

'Where did you get that from?' I asked.

'Found it on the floor in the bedroom,' Shaun replied. 'Why are you seeing a psychologist?'

There was no way I would have left that appointment card on the floor. The only explanation for Shaun having that was that he had been through my purse. If he had done that, I didn't even want to begin to imagine what else he may have done. First my emails and now this?

'Work of course,' I quickly answered.

My heart was thumping and it felt like I could no longer breathe. Shaun had a habit of catching me off guard all the time. I could tell he got a lot of enjoyment out of this too.

'You better not be saying anything about me,' Shaun replied.

There was no way he could find out what I said in these sessions. Or was there? I looked at him, his evil eyes were fixated on me. Shaun was so moody. I turned and walked away feeling his gaze follow me.

Lying in bed later that night I could not sleep. Shaun was sleeping soundly beside me like he didn't have a care in the world. I started to think about my life, I did this so much lately. Did I really want to live like this? I didn't see my friends anymore. I didn't go out anywhere and every move I made was done with total fear. At the same time I had been doubting my thoughts. Was it me overreacting to Shaun's actions? Or was it Shaun meaning to intimidate or scare me with his ways and rules he imposed on me? Either way I should not be feeling like this. Relationships were supposed to improve your life and make it less stressful. I always used to tell myself that if the relationship you were in was easy then it was the right one for you. My current one certainly didn't feel that way. Hopefully Ameera would be able to help me figure out what to do if I continued to see her.

CHAPTER 17

SEXUAL ABUSE

S exual abuse is very hard to talk about at the best of times. Defining the meaning of it is even more difficult. Sometimes you may find yourself in a situation and question whether or not it is in fact abuse or if you're exaggerating it. The scariest part is confiding in someone who may not believe you. I would hesitate to speak with anybody about this topic, even with Ameera, who seemed to be caring and understanding enough to share this difficult topic with.

There was a situation once when I was about eight years old. My brother, sister, cousins and I all went out for lunch with my Grandmother in the city. Dressed in my favourite black and white polka dot skirt and black top, I was very excited. I remember it being a Sunday and that the city was crowded with people that day. Somehow I managed to get lost within the swarms of people and remember panicking when I couldn't see anyone around me who was familiar. The next thing I knew was that I could feel something moving around the outer area of my skirt. I turned around and found myself staring into the face of an older man with curly hair. Thinking that I had imagined what just happened I turned back around, but the same thing happened again. I fled from where I was standing and managed to get to an area which wasn't so flooded with people. Turning back to look in the direction where I had been standing, I could see the man with curly hair watching me from a distance. I burst out crying and that was how my sister and cousin found me. They asked me what happened but I kept silent and didn't say anything. From that day forward I screamed every time I saw what used to be my favourite skirt until it was thrown away. As a child, what happened felt wrong. From the perspective of an adult you know for sure that it was wicked and immoral. This might sound wrong but I sincerely hoped that man was dead so he couldn't do any further harm to other children. The next time he tried something it may have been a lot worse. That man wrecked what was supposed to be a great day and had also given me my first experience of abuse.

As I already mentioned, I was subject to a lot of bullying in high school. This led me to associating myself with the class recluse, Donna. Donna was also teased furiously as she wore thick black-rimmed glasses, walked with a limp and was overweight. We quickly and easily formed a bond as we were both being tormented. Lots of our free time was spent eating junk food and watching Video Hits. Our dream was to go overseas one day and meet lots of famous stars. School got a bit too much for the pair of us which led to us both wagging classes and going into the city to shop. There was one time when after spending the night at my house that Donna refused to go home and was crying furiously. She ran away from my house when her mother came to pick her up. When I asked her what was wrong, she confessed that her father's friend had inappropriately touched her. The advice I gave her was that she should tell someone what had happened to her. I wasn't sure if she ever did or what happened to her as I changed schools shortly after this. I have always felt a bit guilty about not having found a suitable solution to handle this difficult situation.

I was now a few months into my new role (which of course continued to be a constant struggle). One evening, Luke and I were the only ones left in the office working late. The rest of the team were in a training conference that day. These late nights were getting on my nerves, particularly because I was never paid overtime for them.

Just like always, Luke was in a bad mood. I walked into the kitchen to make myself a coffee and thought I'd better bring Luke back one too. On the way back I bent down to hand him his coffee.

'Thanks for that,' said Luke.

This took me by surprise. I was delighted by his positive shift in attitude until I felt something on my leg. It was Luke's hand. I ignored his grotesque gesture as feelings of panic overwhelmed me. I quickly walked back to my desk. Luke had never done anything to me like that before and I was honestly feeling completely repulsed.

'Did you like that?' asked Luke, who was now standing behind me.

Think Carmella, think, I silently said to myself. This wasn't a time to panic. I couldn't speak. I'd seen so many movies on harassment but not one of them came to mind as I tried to think of what I should do. I stood up quickly and made an excuse that I had to go as Shaun was waiting outside. Luke came towards me and it looked like he wanted to embrace me. Grabbing my bag, I successfully avoided what would've been a very uncomfortable and icky situation. As I bounced up, his beady black eyes bore into me as he spoke.

'Carmella, this is our secret,' Luke said. 'If you breathe a word to anybody about what happened I will destroy you both personally and professionally.'

Not knowing what else to do I nodded quickly before I fled out the door.

In the toilet at the train station I heaved the entire contents of my stomach. I felt completely and utterly violated. Tears of anger, frustration and disgust flowed freely from my eyes. Luke was a very powerful man and I knew his threat was not to be taken lightly. Telling Shaun about this could go one of two ways. He would either seek revenge on Luke, or would think I had somehow encouraged the behaviour. I made the decision to keep my mouth shut. This, I felt, was my only option.

CHAPTER 18
MY SO-CALLED FRIEND

At that moment I needed a friend. Things in my professional and personal life had spiralled out of control, and quite frankly I did not know what to do. I decided to call Stephanie, my childhood friend who had recently returned home from being overseas in Europe for many months. During this time Stephanie and I had swapped a few emails, mainly filled with her tales on how her trip was going and the people she had met. I had briefly mentioned Shaun but didn't feel comfortable going into the relationship in great detail for obvious reasons. Stephanie gave the impression that she was not impressed by my new relationship as she barely responded when I twice mentioned that I had met someone. She hadn't even had the chance to meet Shaun, so it wasn't because she had a dislike towards him. I had known Stephanie for most of my life so was surprised when it felt like our friendship was falling apart. Stephanie and I had met in primary school and were close from the get-go. We had a fun type of friendship where we would laugh and stalk our childhood crushes by phone-pranking them. We did however drift apart when we met other friends at university and at work.

I took the opportunity to call Stephanie when Shaun was out fishing with his brother one day. Although I was very anxious about doing so, I thought Stephanie was worth taking a risk for. Shaun hadn't imposed the rule on me not being able to see anyone but I felt he wouldn't be happy if I did.

'Hi, hun! Fancy meeting up for a while?' I asked Stephanie.

I could hear Stephanie hesitate for a moment before she replied. That, in itself, already made me feel uncomfortable. It had been a few weeks since Stephanie's return and I knew that she'd be upset that I hadn't reached out sooner to catch up.

'Oh, if you have the time I guess,' Stephanie replied.

Her attitude was making me wish that I hadn't bothered to call. We ended up agreeing to meet at Café Al Fresco where we both frequently went in our younger days. It was at that time that I knew I shouldn't have bothered.

Stephanie was waiting outside the cafe when I got there. We shared an awkward hug before walking inside.

'So what's been going on?' Stephanie asked as we found a table and took a seat. 'You look like you've lost weight.'

Another thing Stephanie and I had in common was that, once upon a time, we were both very overweight at one point or another in our lives. This was also another thing which brought us together.

'Well, I have been exercising,' I replied.

My response came out a little harsher than expected. I quickly changed the subject to Stephanie's recent trip to Europe. I found myself only half listening as she spoke about her overseas adventures. Stephanie must have noticed and my attention quickly averted as her tone turned harsher.

'Look, Carmella, I know you have a 'so called' busy life, but it bothers me that this is the first time we have seen each other since I returned from Europe,' Stephanie said.

I sighed as I put down the glass of water I was drinking.

'Throughout this whole conversation you have not once asked about my relationship and totally avoided the topic when I emailed you about it. You don't care about me and how I am feeling,' I stated angrily. 'You are so selfish, Stephanie, always have been and always will be. I have to go.'

Stephanie got up, barely saying goodbye, and left me with the coffee bill. Well, that was a waste of time, I thought to myself. I felt more abandoned and alone than ever. Would everyone react that way if I made an effort to reach out to them? On my way out of the cafe I decided to buy some muffins in case Shaun found out I had left the house. This is what my life was becoming.

I was surprised to find Shaun home when I arrived back. I'd expected him to still be fishing with his brother and thought I would be home much before him. He was irritably pacing around the lounge room.

'Where have you been, babe?' asked Shaun, not sounding impressed.

Calling me babe was really beginning to irritate me. I hadn't liked it since Shaun first began calling me that. It was funny that when you become unhappy you think more about what pisses you off.

'Just to the bakery to buy us some muffins,' I replied. 'I got your favourite too, chocolate chip.'

Shaun looked down at the muffins and scowled.

'I've been home for forty-five minutes. We decided not to go fishing after all,' Shaun replied. 'It doesn't take that long to buy a few muffins.'

I froze at his words. If I had known he would be back so early, I would've concocted a more effective cover story.

'I ran into Stephanie while I was there so sat down and had a quick cuppa and chat,' I replied. 'I didn't think I was doing anything out of line. She recently arrived back from Europe.'

Shaun walked up to me, put his face against mine and tightly gripped my arm.

'I have told you repeatedly that I don't want you seeing any friends, especially without me being there,' Shaun replied angrily.

This must be a new rule, I thought to myself. I knew of the no drinking one but not this one.

'I didn't expect to see her there and it had been so long since I'd caught up with her,' I replied. 'I didn't think you would mind. Why aren't I allowed to see my friends anyway?'

'I don't even know Stephanie,' Shaun said. 'You are never to do anything like that again, understand?'

I hurriedly nodded as his grip on my arm tightened. Shaun knew of Stephanie as I had mentioned her, being a childhood friend and all. I knew trying to explain that Stephanie had been overseas would be a pointless exercise. Physically hurting me was something new. The look in Shaun's eyes frightened me so much and I wanted him to let go of me.

'Good! I'm glad we have that sorted,' Shaun said. 'Now, go to the kitchen and get me a beer so I can have one with those muffins.'

I put the muffins down on the table and walked to the kitchen. What I had done was particularly silly. I had risked making Shaun angry for someone I had thought was a friend. Of course there was no reason for Shaun's anger but that was the way he rolled and I really should've known this.

My friendship with Stephanie ended that day and that was the last time I saw her. Although I must admit I didn't fully blame her and would probably still be friends with her today if it hadn't been for Shaun. In my 'old' life I would definitely have seen her a lot sooner than a few weeks after her return from overseas.

Before I walked back to the lounge room with Shaun's beer, I spat in his bottle. I smiled to myself and felt a sense of satisfaction. That was his gift in return for gripping my arm so roughly.

All of which led to a very 'colourful' session in Ameera's office the following week, as I bemoaned my faithless ex-friend and my life with my controlling, unsympathetic life partner. I used up a significant proportion of Ameera's ample supply of tissues, crying, I think more in anger and frustration than actual sadness. In a sense, I was already beyond mourning this unhealthy, poisoned relationship.

I looked up to see Ameera fixing me with a steady, meaningful gaze.

'What?' I asked her, puzzled.

'Carmella, what did you think Stephanie was going to do for you? Give you a license to get your life back on track? Give you permission to leave?' she asked softly.

'Well, err. I don't know … Maybe at least ask me about my relationship?' I replied.

'You don't need a crutch, Carmella,' Ameera responded.

'No, of course. I know that,' I said.

'Do you? Do you really?' Ameera said, with her disconcerting quizzical look. 'If that was the case, why seek out a friend you must have known deep down wouldn't, or couldn't support you?'

'I don't think I thought it through that thoroughly,' I replied.

'Consciously. But unconsciously, I think you were simply ticking off the boxes, seeking support from a friend while knowing at some level you wouldn't get it,' Ameera concluded.

I sighed. 'I don't know what else to do.'

The quizzical look didn't abate.

'I think you do, Carmella,' Ameera resumed. 'You have the strength in yourself to make this decision and to follow through with it. While it's nice to have friends, you and you alone are going to need to make this decision. Only you can make this change in your life and, at some level you know you have the power to make it happen.'

I stared at her, hating her at that moment, knowing she was right.

CHAPTER 19
CONCERT AND PHONES

Over the coming weeks, Shaun's obsessive behaviour became worse and worse. I felt as though I needed permission for everything. It felt this way because it was true. My life no longer belonged to me.

Out of the blue my nephew, Emilio, rang me. I was feeling particularly down that day when thinking of what my life had become so it was a lovely feeling to hear his voice. Emilio was my sister's son, five years old and in grade prep. I had been close with him since the day he was born. Strikingly handsome with dark hair and eyes, he was a small male version of me. He advised me, his voice filled with tremendous excitement, that his grade prep class was having a concert and that he would love me to be there. I told him I would be delighted to go and wouldn't miss it for the world. I called my mum to find out if she would also be attending and we arranged that we would go together. It didn't even cross my mind that saying 'yes' to this would cause issues, but boy was I wrong.

It was Friday night and once again I'd had a long week. When I got home from work, I crawled straight into bed with a book. I didn't feel like eating which was normal for me these days. A few minutes later, I heard Shaun walk into the room. His body language gave me negative vibes and I could tell that he was bothered by something.

'So, I heard you're going to your nephew's concert,' he told me.

'Yes,' I replied. 'I didn't think I was doing anything wrong with saying I'd go.'

My defensive tone when answering Shaun's questions became the norm nowadays. Lately if Shaun raised something with me, it meant that he had an issue with it.

'You do know my sister's ex who is also the grade prep teacher will be there, don't you?' Shaun asked.

I felt his fingers which slowly crawled up my back to my neck over and over. Shaun's sister's daughter, Beatrice, whom I'd met at Shaun's parents' house, went to the same school as Emilio and they were in the same class. Anita, Shaun's sister, had once had a relationship with Mr Greenwood who was Emilio's and Beatrice's teacher. He cheated on her during their time together and Anita had apparently never recovered from this. Shaun, it appeared, had also not been able to forget what happened to his sister and claimed that if he ever saw Mr Greenwood again that he would beat him up.

'To be honest it did not even cross my mind,' I said. 'And why would it? I'm going to the concert for Emilio's sake and nobody else's.'

I could feel Shaun's hand as it continued to rub up and down my back. Throughout this entire conversation, my eyes were fixated on a small black dot on the wall. I suddenly felt Shaun's hand grab my hair. It didn't hurt but the gesture felt threatening, and I felt frightened and vulnerable. This was also the second time he had touched me in an abusive way. It felt a little rough and I saw it as some sort of a warning. Then came the bombshell. He told me there was no way I would be going to the concert especially because he wouldn't be. In fact, he said he couldn't believe I would ever dream of going after what happened to his sister. I started to analyse the situation in my mind and didn't understand what attending the concert had to do with his sister's life. I told him that I still wanted to go and it was then that the grip on my hair tightened and he raised his voice.

'WHAT IS MORE IMPORTANT? MAKING ME HAPPY OR GOING TO THAT STUPID CONCERT?' Shaun asked, yelling at the same time.

I couldn't believe what was happening. It felt like I was in a nightmare. The only choice I had at that moment was to say I wouldn't be attending the concert. It was the only way I knew how to end the situation and for Shaun to loosen his grip on my hair. Surrendering to Shaun's every demand was so typical of me these days. Who knows what he would've done if I had stood up for myself. I told Shaun I wouldn't be going to the concert and he embraced me. It felt like I had lost full control over my entire life yet again. There was nothing I wanted more at that moment than to get away from Shaun. The problem was always the same, I wasn't sure how to do this.

It didn't take me long to figure out that Shaun had shared what had happened with Shauna. I received a call from her the next day to talk about it.

'Shaun's so protective of you and his sister,' said Shauna. 'He has always been like that with all the women in his life. You're a very lucky lady.'

I was at a loss for words and didn't reply to her stupidity. Trying to explain that I would've loved to have gone to the concert would've been a waste of time on my part. She would surely have refused to hear any part of this, explaining that her son was right to have felt this way. Standing up for me against her son would've also been taboo.

'Mr Greenwood is a bad man. It's fair that Shaun would not want you associating with him,' Shauna continued.

I was defeated. I wasn't sure what response I was looking for in Shauna. She hated my guts.

The concert was apparently fantastic as Shauna, who had attended, hadn't tried to hide this fact from me. Poor Emilio was very disappointed that I didn't attend the concert but understood about the 'nasty flu' that I had apparently caught two days prior to the event.

One night in bed, Shaun told me he wanted to buy himself the latest Apple iPhone and that I should keep his old one.

'I don't want your iPhone. My phone works perfectly fine,' I advised.

'Would you rather I buy you a new phone and keep my old one?' Shaun asked.

I stared at him for a moment and tried to work out what he was playing at.

'No, I don't want your phone or a new one,' I continued. 'I already have one and don't need another one.'

'Just hang on to your crappy old phone then,' he said.

This conversation about phones went on for quite a while. Shaun was extremely persistent about the matter so I decided to ask him why.

'I truly love you and only want you to have the best of everything,' he said.

I decided to agree as the phone Shaun offered me was a few models later than my current one and had some additional features. Did I believe the line about him loving me? No, it was more about possession in my opinion. What was the harm in the phone though?

By the next week, Shaun had a new phone and gave me his old one. He inserted my sim card into it and showed me how to use it. He seemed extremely happy that I now had his phone. We had a good rest of the day watching movies and talking. By the end of the day I was feeling relaxed. Shaun lent over to kiss me right before going to sleep.

'Oh, by the way, I have also inserted a tracking device in

your phone so I always know where you are,' Shaun said. 'Some ideas you've recently had including going to that stupid concert have worried me. I won't be as concerned for your safety now.'

I stared straight into Shaun's eyes and was about to reply when he laughed.

'Oh Carmella, you are so gullible,' he said. 'As if I would ever do something like that.'

Shaun shook his head and switched the light off then laughed again. I wasn't sure what to believe but I knew I should be careful about where I carried that phone.

CHAPTER 20
THE INJURY

Things were extremely awkward with Luke after our 'late night incident' and the bullying did not cease. Every morning before I entered the work building my heart pounded and my breath caught in my throat. Would I ever be alone with Luke in the office again? What would I do if he tried something a second time? I had feelings of anxiety which I had never felt in any job before and this wasn't due to the role being fast-paced and busy.

One particular morning, I was about to walk into work. The air was fresh and crisp but I felt as if I was suffocating. I gulped, trying to inhale one deep breath before going in. My body was definitely struggling with my life's current stress and anxiety. The day was going to be frantically busy. There was a teleconference scheduled in the morning with one company and then an in-person meeting in the afternoon with a second group of clients. We were partnering with both of these clients to organise student events. I closed my eyes and tried to relax one last time before facing the day. It did not work and I realised I had no other choice but to go in.

When I walked into the office, I could tell by the look on Luke's face that he was angry about something which was the usual. Luke's moods and behaviour were unspoken of in the office and I didn't feel as though I could raise these issues with any of the other team members. I was heartened to see that Sheila was already in the office. Luke's and my eyes met in the light streaming from the window which sat above Luke's desk. I tried to start the day off in a positive mood by striking up a conversation. I knew what Luke did was wrong but trying to forget about it seemed like the right thing to do, especially until my placement ceased.

'Good morning, Luke,' I said brightly.

This was my usual morning greeting to him. I received a grunt in reply before he spoke.

'Make sure that hotline is up and running for this morning's conference as the clients are dialling in at 10.00 am,' Luke said.

I had done three trial runs with setting up the hotline so was quite confident that there would be no hiccups. Luke had drummed it into my head a million times how important this conference was. It was with a high profile client from Brazil who was looking to partner with an

Australian company to run their annual student graduation event. There was a lot of money at stake for this.

The time was now 9.00 am so I went about setting up the meeting room for our internal team and then the setup of the hotline. By 9.30 am, the room and the hotline were both prepared and ready to go. My nerves finally began to calm down a little.

Luke walked in the meeting room at 9.45 am ahead of the rest of the team members. He asked me to dial into the meeting early. I had the code with me so was able to do that right away. With trembling hands, I began to plug in the code. To my dismay, the hotline now appeared to not be working. There was no dial tone. I turned to Luke, and with a rapidly beating heart told him what I had discovered.

'The hotline isn't working,' I said.

I felt sweat forming on my fingers as I anxiously laced them through one another.

'What do you mean?' Luke asked, his face filled with anger.

'There is no dial tone,' I replied.

Luke looked at me, his face was bright red and looked as though it was about to explode. For a split second there I envisioned his feral face expanding and blowing up and thought how great that would be.

'FUUUUUUUUUCK!' he exclaimed before he stormed off.

There I was, left standing all alone. I felt extremely useless and beaten down. Nobody had ever sworn at me like that in the workplace before. It was both rude and utterly unprofessional. I felt like I was about to have a nervous breakdown. It was at that moment that Sheila walked into the meeting room. There was an unspoken understanding between Sheila and I. I could tell she knew I was being bullied by Luke but none of us said anything to each other about it. I told her what happened and she took a look at the setup of our 'state of the art' hotline.

'You forgot to turn the power back on, after it went into sleep mode,' Sheila told me.

My nerves had got the better of me. It was so unlike me to forget something as simple as that. I thanked her for coming to my aid and in return she told me that the room looked great.

It was right on 10.00 am and the rest of the team entered the room, led by Luke. Many of my colleagues were full of compliments. I couldn't bring myself to say anything in return except to provide a nod of thanks. The international company ended up signing a contract with us. I never received an apology from Luke for the way he spoke to me that morning and nor did I expect one.

The rest of the day continued and I felt sick to my stomach. I wanted to call it a day by saying I wasn't feeling well and going home. Who knew what I would face at home though? Shaun's movements were so unpredictable that he could either be at home or work. Going home to him wasn't appealing either. I would've loved to have gone shopping but was extremely suspicious of now having to carry Shaun's old phone with its 'maybe installed' tracking device. Instead, I stuck around for the second important meeting of the day. I focused on the task at hand with a smile on my face, going through my checklist of jobs that needed to be done prior to the meeting. Luke made no attempt to speak to me as he saw me greeting clients, showing them to their seats and handing them a folder of papers for the meeting. The folders were of course hole-punched and perfectly lined up. Who would have thought that perfect hole-punching would ever be ranked a top priority on the important list? Things seemed to be on track until Sheila walked up to me.

'Luke wanted me to ask you when the tea, coffee and hot fudge brownies will arrive,' Sheila said.

I looked at her blankly before I replied.

'Luke told me not to worry about it as he would be asking Danielle to arrange the catering,' I said.

Danielle was Luke's Executive Assistant who seemed to do no wrong in Luke's eyes.

A look of worry passed over Sheila's face which caused me to become concerned.

'Come on,' she said. 'Let's see what we can find in the kitchen downstairs.'

We both rushed to the kitchen and managed to pull together a few mugs with some instant coffee, tea bags and sugar, but unfortunately there were no hot fudge brownies. When our tray was set up we both rushed back upstairs. In my efforts of trying to do this quickly, my foot got caught on one of the steps and I toppled backwards and fell. My back was in excruciating pain. I began to cry. I wasn't sure what I was crying about more; the pain in my back or the stress I was feeling. Sheila ran back down the stairs but I told her to deliver the tea and coffee to the meeting. She promised to hurry back as soon as she could to help me up. I watched Sheila's red jacket as she continued back up the stairs holding the tray. I remained sitting at the bottom of the stairs wondering how pathetic I must've looked. I felt completely crushed both inside and out. As promised, Sheila came back to help me. She also had a taxi voucher for me so I could go home. Sheila pulled me up and escorted me to the closest taxi rank. She advised that our clients were grateful for the tea and coffee which I guess was at least something. The next thing she said firmly stuck in my mind.

'You don't want to work with Luke, Carmella,' Sheila said. 'You and I both know what a monster he is.'

Right then the penny dropped. The look in her eyes said it all. The late nights and early starts at work, Sheila had also been abused by Luke. Just as I was about to speak, Sheila laid a hand on my arm which I took as a sign to remain silent. I gave Sheila a hug before I struggled to get in a taxi.

On my way home I had feelings of being alone yet again. Once upon a time this was something I would have definitely phoned a friend about. All that closeness I had once felt with my friends had now disappeared. I felt like I had no close friends left other than Sarah who I never saw anymore. The outside world also looked so lonely with no traffic and cloudy skies with no birds. I thought about how much I hated my life at present and not for the first time.

Later that week, yet again, Ameera bore the brunt of my 'unrequited hate' and frustration. I was lucky to have scored a phone appointment with her while Shaun was at work.

'I can't win, Ameera! I am trapped! And there's no let up! It's either Luke at work or Shaun at home,' I raged. 'My life is one big nightmare.'

'It sounds very difficult. And it's natural that you're upset,' Ameera soothed.

'But there's no way out!' I continued, blinking the tears of anger out of my eyes. 'I am hopelessly trapped!'

Through the phone I knew Ameera wore her calm, quizzical stare, that by now, I was all too familiar with.

'Do you believe that, Carmella? Or is it simply easier for you to assume that belief?' she asked.

I paused.

'Why would I do that? Lie to myself?' I asked.

'Aren't the benefits obvious?' she responded.

I was puzzled.

Ameera continued, 'In some ways, many people find the pain of the inertia and remaining in a bad or unhealthy situation less than the fear and anxiety associated with taking action to change it.'

I tried to process her words. Was this really true?

CHAPTER 21

NO GYM OR PILATES

For now, I was going nowhere. I had no other choice but to stay home injured. The time at home had been both positive and negative so far. I loved the time on my own as it gave me a lot of time to think. There were times I didn't love it so much, such as when Shaun was home or I had unexpected visits from Shauna. The times with Shauna were always so awkward as I knew she didn't like me. Most of her visits took place when Shaun was at work. I wouldn't have been in the least surprised if Shaun had asked Shauna to check up on me. When Shauna visited she never arrived empty-handed and always came with homemade food claiming she wanted to look after me. Call me a cynic but I didn't believe that for a second.

I had made the decision to leave my fixed-term role with Luke and make an early return to my substantive role. My former manager, Naomi, had no problems with this and was in fact excited about my return, explaining that there were a number of important projects coming up. Naomi was so keen for my return that she did all the paperwork with Luke regarding my early release. The reason I gave Naomi for my sooner-than-expected return date was, 'I just didn't fit in.' My treatment at work by Luke professionally and sexually had shattered my confidence and left me broken. What made it even more difficult to understand was that nobody had ever done anything about Luke's appalling behaviour. I had a brief conversation with Sheila and asked her if she would be willing to speak up about what had happened to me and what was currently happening to her. Sheila opened up to me and confirmed that my suspicions were correct. Luke was abusing her in a sexual way. She also advised me that she didn't want anybody else to know and I respected her decision. I was frightened, but made the decision to report what happened by writing to the Human Resources Department of the company. Mustering up my courage to do so, I wrote a document containing all the events that occurred with Luke including all the bullying I was put through as well as the sexual abuse. I trusted the company to keep what I reported as confidential. By not taking action, it made Luke think it was OK to treat women this way. I felt the need to take action in my life as a whole and this seemed like a great start. What would come out of this, I wasn't sure, but I felt satisfied that I took charge. I definitely would not be sharing this with Shaun.

Life of course also continued to be extremely challenging with Shaun. I wanted to get my mind to the level of sharpness it was once at. Reporting Luke's behaviour had definitely given me that first step in believing I could do this. Shaun's constant texts and calls to me throughout the day, when he was working, were utterly annoying and hugely distracting. This made it difficult for me to focus on anything. I was more than sure that he was checking up on me rather than being concerned for my well-being. What he expected me to be up to, I wasn't sure. It was painful for me to even walk.

Shaun and I had an argument the next day. He decided to take the next day off from work. I valued my alone time, barring Shaun's constant phone calls and texts, so was disappointed. We spent the majority of the day watching movies and listening to music which was fine. We then started to talk about exercise and my recovery. My idea of exercise before having met Shaun was going to the gym six days a week and going for a run after work every night. The level of confidence I achieved when joining the gym was something I couldn't even begin to explain. I lost twenty kilograms and I felt and looked amazing. I told Shaun that once my back began to improve, I hoped to join a gym and do some Pilates classes. My doctor had informed me that this was a good way to help strengthen your body core muscles.

'Why would you want to do that?' Shaun asked.

I looked at him, believing I had just explained myself, but repeated my reasons for this anyway.

'To become fit again and I heard Pilates classes strengthen your core muscles,' I replied.

Shaun looked at me like I'd just slapped him in the face. Judging by past conversations with him, I couldn't even begin to imagine what his issue with this might've been.

'You do realise that there are men at gyms and Pilates classes, don't you?' he asked.

I'm not sure if this was a trick question so took my time to think before I replied.

'Yes, I do Shaun, but I'm not going there to speak with men,' I said. 'I need to get fit and strengthen my back.'

This response seemed to get him angry.

'I don't want you to go,' he said. 'You'll be wearing leggings and we all know how tight they are. Other men will be able to see the outline of your vagina.'

I looked at him and knew very well that this could go into argument territory. Men staring at the outline of my vagina? It was unheard of. This was not a good time for me to be getting into these conversations. My full recovery was still a few weeks away and I wanted to focus all my energy on that. I was stuck dealing with Shaun during this time whether I liked it or not. What I desperately wanted to say to him would not be taken lightly. I was genuinely beginning to think he was a psychopath. My life with a psychopath. This had to be the most pathetic thing I had heard coming from him and there had been some pretty tragic statements and rules from him. I told Shaun that I was not presently interested in discussing this matter. Once again, this response did not sit well with him as this was all he talked about for the next two hours. I fought back a little but decided not to waste what little strength I had on this discussion. Going to bed early was the only way to get away from this situation.

A few days later, Shaun brought up the topic of the gym and Pilates classes again.

'Look,' I said, 'if it's that important to you I won't go.'

This would hopefully shut him up. Shaun seemed pleased by my response and said that he knew I would understand his point and was happy that we'd finally cleared up the situation. He also said that he discussed it with some family members who also agreed with him. There was no doubt in my mind that he had discussed this with Shauna. Gee, I wished she would mind her own business. If I had raised this situation with someone, I could confidently say that they would think there was nothing wrong with me attending the gym or Pilates classes. A normal person would've surely taken my side. Danger bells were definitely ringing again which I was glad I wasn't deaf to.

Over the next few weeks, with lots of rest, my back began to improve. I bought myself a resistance band online and did some of my own exercises to strengthen my core muscles. When I was able to drive again, I also ended up visiting a physiotherapist named Rita for some dry needling. Shaun was OK with me seeing her as she was a woman. During one of my sessions, Rita asked me if I'd be interested in undertaking a Pilates class. I took up this offer by saying that I would love to. My next appointment would be a class instead of a one-on-one. Shaun couldn't be around to check on me as he had to work. The class was fabulous and significantly helped my road to recovery. Men were also in attendance. I was able to have decent conversations with them, and guess what? We weren't hitting on one another. Shaun never found out about this or about the hot pink leggings I wore. I saw this as being a small victory for me.

CHAPTER 22
RETURNING TO WORK AND LIST OF RULES

My back was finally starting to heal, which meant I could slowly return to work. This was an absolute relief for me as I had had enough of either Shaun being home from work, or badgering me on the days when he wasn't there. It was going to be nice being in adult company other than Shaun's or Shauna's. I was also returning to my former position at the Student Glamour event company which was a huge comfort. I was so excited to be back with my old team members again. I never heard from Luke in all the time I was off from work and hadn't expected to. If I ever saw him in the building I would do my best to avoid him or take the stairs if he were waiting for the lift. The thought of even seeing him again repulsed me, let alone the thought of talking to him.

It seemed so safe and familiar as I walked into work that first morning. This was the first time I had been happy in weeks. During my time off, my former team sent me flowers and a box of chocolates which of course was a gesture of inspiration to get better. Shaun, being the way he was, threw my gifts away as male team members had signed my card.

My eyes widened with surprise as I walked into the office that morning. There was a large table covered with all my favourite breakfast pastries including croissants, Danishes and muffins which were accompanied by freshly squeezed orange juice and brewed coffee. Cheryl, Kristen and some of my other work colleagues were standing around the table holding a sign which read 'Welcome Back'. I stood there and almost burst into tears at the work that had been done to organise all of this. It seemed like such a long time ago that anybody had done something this thoughtful for me. After the formalities of a Welcome Back speech and hugs from my team members, I settled into a conversation with Cheryl and Kristen.

'We're so happy to have you back,' said Cheryl. 'We couldn't believe it when we heard you had injured yourself.'

'I know,' I said. 'It was horrible.'

'What was it like to work for Luke?' Cheryl asked, biting into a croissant. 'There's word around the traps that he can be very demanding.'

There was no easy way to answer this question. I didn't

want to lie to Cheryl and Kristen but also didn't want to get into what happened at this particular moment, especially in reporting Luke's behaviour.

'Let's just say that I'm very happy to be back,' I said.

That seemed like the best answer in response to their question. Cheryl and Kristen knew that more had happened but didn't push the situation.

I couldn't be happier on my first day back at work. It was so great to be back with my old team and it made me realise that who you work with is more important than the work you do. Having said that, the project I'd been given to work on was a ripper and involved organising a Scholarship Program for disadvantaged university students. I was so engrossed in my work that when I glanced at my watch I was surprised to see that it was almost midday. Feeling hungry, I went and grabbed my sandwich out of the fridge and walked over to Cheryl and Kristen.

'Do you want to eat lunch together?' I asked.

'Absolutely,' said Cheryl. 'You're not eating that though,' she continued, pointing at my sandwich. 'The team is taking you out to Yum Cha. We have booked your favourite place and we haven't been there since you left.'

I stood there trying to look excited rather than panicky. This was totally unexpected after the morning tea which was organised for me. My promise to Shaun about not being in the company of other men when he wasn't there stuck in my head. I wasn't sure how I could decline the lunch so I wondered whether I should take the risk.

'The booking is for 12.30 pm at *Little China* so we

should go,' Kristen said. 'I'll go and round up Andy, Naomi and Steve.'

I made an excuse about having to go to the ladies' room first and that I'd meet them there. Everyone else I knew would attend without having to worry or deal with someone like Shaun. I carefully thought this through for the next ten minutes taking in deep breaths as I did so. Grabbing my bag, I decided to risk it.

Walking through the streets, my anxiety levels escalated. I kept glancing over my shoulder not entirely sure what I was looking for. In some way I expected Shaun to appear there. When my phone rang I wasn't in the least bit surprised to see his number appear. I had no other choice but to answer because if I didn't who knows what he'd do.

'Hello,' I said.

'Where are you?' Shaun asked. 'It sounds bustling.'

'Just taking a walk through the city,' I replied.

'Why aren't you eating lunch?' Shaun asked.

I slowly exhaled.

'I needed some air,' I said.

'How can you have time to walk and eat lunch? You only get a half hour.' He paused before continuing. 'Are you going out for lunch?'

I found that I was unable to lie. Firstly, I was frightened to do so and secondly I knew that Shaun would find out. He had his ways.

'My team have organised a welcome back lunch for me,' I softly said.

I could feel Shaun's anger pulsating through the phone before he even spoke.

'You'd better not go, Carmella,' Shaun responded threateningly. 'So help me God, if you do I will drag you out of that damn restaurant.'

I promised not to go to the lunch before I hung up. My day was going so well until this. I sent texts to both Cheryl and Kristen telling them I wasn't feeling well and that I had decided to head home. I barely remembered that train ride home as I was angry and frustrated for the entire duration.

When I walked through the door Shaun didn't even look my way.

'There is a whiteboard attached to the fridge with the promises you've made to me,' Shaun said, biting into an apple. 'It might be good for you to read them and refresh your memory. Go and have a look.'

I walked into the kitchen where the whiteboard sat prominently fixed to the centre of the fridge door. Slowly, I read what it said.

List of Carmella's Promises:
· *No drinking alcohol in the presence of anyone other than Shaun*
· *No going to the gym*
· *No attending Pilates classes*
· *No going out with friends anywhere, especially male ones*
· *No watching male nudity in movies or on the internet*
· *No wearing short dresses or outfits which show my cleavage*

· *No flirting with the opposite sex*
· *No going anywhere unless Shaun knows where I am*
· *Have my phone on me at all times*

I desperately wished he would choke on his apple.

CHAPTER 23

AT THE RACES

In bed one night, Shaun told me that he wanted us to do something fun. I agreed thinking it might actually be nice to go out and drink something alcoholic. He was, after all, the only person I was allowed to do that with. After a lengthy discussion we decided that horse racing might be fun. Shaun had never been before and the last time I went I was a little girl. Shaun was excited which sort of made me feel happy. I was hoping the happiness would at least last until our day at the races ended.

The next day I booked us two tickets to Flemington races for two weeks' time. I also had time to shop online for a new dress. The dress I chose was red and slightly slinky but with, naturally, my cleavage safely hidden. I also purchased a red floral fascinator to match it.

It was races day and I was getting ready. When my

outfit was on and my make-up and hair were done, I made my way to the lounge room. Shaun was waiting for me, looking smart and elegant in a black suit and tie. I told him he looked fantastic which he did. Shaun didn't return the compliment or in any way comment on my appearance which disappointed me. I took this as an opportunity to ask him if he liked the way I looked, and in response, he grabbed the car keys and said he didn't want to miss the first race. I shrugged off my paranoid feelings and told myself that he couldn't have heard my question.

We arrived at Flemington a bit later than expected due to heavy traffic, but still had time to place a bet in the first race. I looked around and absolutely loved the atmosphere of the day. There were lots of people dressed in beautiful attire and Shaun and I really did fit in well. We found a position close to the racetrack and watched the horses run. I didn't know a lot about horses, or jockeys for that matter, but chose my lucky number which was two. To my delight number two won the race.

'Nice fluke,' Shaun said as he tore up his ticket.

'Better than a fluke,' I playfully replied. 'I beat you.'

We decided to put on a bet in the next race too. This time I looked at the Form Guide and decided to go with the jockey who wore my favourite colour which was red. The horse was number twelve. We took our same position by the racetrack and watched the race. I was surprised when my horse won again. This one was also paying a lot of money which made me even happier. Shaun stormed off and I found myself chasing him trying to find out what the problem was. Surely he couldn't be angry because I won two races? When catching up with him, I asked Shaun what was wrong and if he was angry at something.

'I'm not angry,' Shaun said.

His body language told me something different. Was there ever a time when Shaun wasn't angry?

'Well, you seem it,' I replied.

Shaun kept denying it and I saw no point in discussing the matter further.

I decided to change the subject and asked Shaun if he would like to sit down and have some lunch. We found a place on the lawn and took a seat. Shaun told me that he would go and get us some lunch and that I should save us a spot on the lawn. Shaun returned with two flutes of champagne and some sandwiches. He handed me a flute of champagne.

'Cheers to a great day,' Shaun said.

I held out my flute to salute Shaun's and before I knew it I had an entire glass of champagne tipped all over my dress. I stared at Shaun in shock, who was laughing at the situation.

'Oops, sorry,' he said.

I felt the tears forming in my eyes which began to drip down my cheeks. Shaun did that on purpose and I found myself wondering why he would want to hurt me like that. I stared down at my dress as the champagne soaked into it. I found myself becoming very angry.

'You did that on purpose,' I softly said, feeling defeated.

This made Shaun laugh even harder.

'You can't be serious,' he said.

When I didn't reply, Shaun became withdrawn.

'Let's go home, I don't want to stay here anymore,' he said.

I didn't argue and we made our way to the car. Shaun succeeded in ruining my day yet again and I didn't feel like staying at the races with him either. This scenario was also becoming a ritual, being that if Shaun didn't like something he would storm off.

There was very little chatter on the way and at our arrival home. After removing my alcohol-drenched dress and showering, I occupied myself with a good novel and a text conversation with Sarah for the majority of the afternoon. Sarah was still happily in love with Sam but taking things slow. I could not even begin to advise her how smart she was in doing that. I started to feel a little better as the afternoon went on.

During dinner that evening, Shaun broke the ice.

'Stop being a baby, Carmella,' he said. 'What happened today was pretty funny.'

Shaun even made a point of leaning across the table and pretending to tip his beverage over me. This antic was repeated a few times until I asked him to stop. Shaun could be so immature. I wished he would fall face first right onto his dinner plate.

'Well, I thought it was funny,' Shaun said.

We ate in silence until he started to talk again.

'I did you a favour,' Shaun said. 'You looked like a fat whore in that dress. There were so many people looking at you that I became embarrassed for you.'

I couldn't believe what I'd just heard. Had I even heard him correctly? This was definitely the meanest thing he had ever said to me. Nobody had called me fat since I was the second largest child in primary school. As for being a whore, I'd never, ever been called that in my entire life. There was no way to describe the hurt I felt as I heard these words. I wanted a nice day out and to look appealing for my partner and this was the way I was treated in return. A burning anger built up within me. I made the decision to give Shaun the silent treatment. This time his nastiness had gone way too far.

The next few days were spent trying to avoid Shaun. I left to go to work in the morning when he was asleep and came home only speaking to him when I absolutely had to. Shaun called and sent numerous texts when I was at work, furiously apologising saying that he was joking. In my opinion, calling someone a fat whore was not my idea of a joke. I generally have a great sense of humour and am one of the first people who can take a joke. The truth was I didn't think Shaun was at all sorry. I also saw his texts as being another excuse to keep further tabs on my movements. I ignored his efforts and found myself feeling great pleasure in doing so.

CHAPTER 24
TEDDY BEAR

Work was extremely busy and I had multiple deadlines to meet for clients. Our company was working on an event for an author who had recently released a self-help book for students. I was really excited about this event as I'd read the book and believed it would be of a great benefit to young people who were commencing their tertiary studies. There were so many students who needed guidance and the advice this book gave was invaluable. Plus, I was also supervising a new team of four people which was taking up a lot of my time. They were unfamiliar with the way the system worked and therefore had a lot of questions throughout the day.

Since the argument when Shaun labelled me as a 'fat whore', his texts when I was at work were relentless. I had found it very difficult to forgive him as to me this was a huge insult. I believed he knew he was wrong on this occasion. Shaun's response to that was that no matter what happened between us that I should always be readily available to answer his messages. I let him have his opinion as there was no use arguing with him.

Not being able to constantly reply to all of Shaun's texts while I was at work began to impact our fragile relationship even more, if that were at all possible. It became a bit of a tradition for me to outline my day when arriving home from work. Shaun liked to compare the times of texts being sent which weren't answered to what I was doing at the time. He didn't admit to this but I knew that was exactly what he was doing. Shaun would look at his texts and ask if I had a meeting at the time I didn't reply to one. I jokingly and with a lot of sarcasm suggested to him that I should print him out copies of my daily schedule. Shaun agreed that this was a great idea. Making this suggestion was a huge mistake on my part. There was no way that I could agree to this. Firstly, my work was my business and didn't have anything to do with him. Secondly, my work schedule constantly shifted on a daily basis. I didn't want to think about how Shaun would react if I couldn't respond to a text when he thought I was free.

It was the day before the big event and I was furiously tying up loose ends. I suddenly felt a tap on my shoulder and turned to face Cheryl.

'Uh, Carmella, I think Shaun is here,' she said.

I quickly turned to face her, not believing what I was hearing. Shaun knew not to turn up to my work and especially unannounced. He had his rules with socialising with men on a personal level but being at work in the office was a different story.

'Where is he?' I asked.

No words were necessary when Cheryl pointed over to where Shaun was standing. I couldn't believe my eyes. In Shaun's hands was the largest teddy bear I had ever seen with the words 'I miss you' scrawled across its chest. Slowly I walked over to Shaun, smiling at my colleagues who were looking over at me. As I walked past I heard quite a few snickers. I wanted to fall through the floor and reappear when the office was empty.

'What are you doing here?' I quietly asked Shaun when I had finally approached him.

Shaun smiled widely at me before responding.

'Well, since you never respond to my texts, I thought having this at your desk would constantly remind you to do so,' Shaun whispered back. 'It's also another way of saying sorry for the other day.'

'You could've handled this situation another way,' I replied. 'I am so embarrassed.'

One of the first things Shaun and I discussed when we first got together was how much I valued my privacy at work and how important it was to me. Now this situation had totally given my colleagues something to constantly gossip about. Shaun and I continued to have a heated discussion in whispered voices. We were both wearing smiles on our faces so nobody knew that our discussion was far from a happy one. Shaun ended up leaving in a huff and I walked back to my desk holding this large bear I could barely carry. The disadvantage with working in an open-plan environment is that everybody saw what had just happened. I heard further snickering and thought that if I were looking at myself that I would be laughing too. Cheryl and Kristen both questioned the visit once I was back at my desk. I told them that Shaun had been away for work the last couple of weeks and had missed me. It was the best response I could come up with in that very moment which I thought was a pretty good one.

By the time Shaun came home from work that night I was already in bed with the door closed. I heard him slowly walk through the door and felt his presence standing over our bed.

'Can we talk?' Shaun asked.

I sat up in bed and glared at him. Not feeling like talking, I asked him what about and if it could wait. Ignoring me, he sat on the bed and began to talk anyway.

'I'm sorry,' Shaun said. 'I felt that turning up to your work was the only real way I could get your attention and for you to accept my apology. I even took an extended lunch break so I could deliver the present to you myself.'

He sounded so proud of himself as he said this. I responded by telling him that all I wanted to do was go to sleep. Shaun seemed to accept my response this time as I didn't remember anything but falling into a deep sleep.

The next morning I woke up to the delicious smell of freshly brewed coffee. I got myself out of bed and walked to the kitchen where Shaun was busily preparing breakfast.

Shaun said good morning to me and turned back to the scrambled eggs he was making. It was very unusual for Shaun to be cooking a hot breakfast as mornings were very busy for both of us. Shaun also loved to sleep in, with the exception of the twittering of the birds. I took a seat at the kitchen table. Shaun poured me a glass of orange juice and put a plate of eggs in front of me. I found it very hard to resist and Shaun knew that scrambled eggs were my absolute favourite. Picking up a fork I began to eat. Shaun also took a seat at the table.

'I'm sorry for yesterday,' Shaun began.

I still hadn't recovered from his 'gesture of kindness' but felt I had to respond to him.

'You know the way I feel about my privacy,' I replied. 'I especially like to keep my work and home life separate and you knew this.'

Shaun seemed deflated by my response but kept talking.

'It's the only way I knew how to make you pay attention,' Shaun said.

I went on to explain that it was very difficult for me to respond to all of his texts as I was always busy at work. Shaun didn't seem to understand what I was saying and once again insisted he should be considered the first priority in my life. Like on many occasions, I found myself beginning to doubt my way of responding to issues. Should everything in my life be secondary to Shaun, including my responsibilities at work? Surely he couldn't be this needy for my attention? No matter what my opinion was, I had to ensure I was able to respond to the majority of Shaun's texts as much as I could when working. I had to prevent anything like the 'teddy bear' incident ever happening again. It did also cross my mind that this was the first act of kindness that Shaun had shown me in quite some time.

CHAPTER 25

FLIRTING WITH WOMEN AND THE BIRTHDAY PARTY

T he act of kindness was a one-off situation. Shaun's behaviour became worse over time and I felt no better than a piece of dirt he would tread on with his dirty sneaker.

Shaun had always had a way with women. He reeled them in with what he considered to be his sweetness and charms, particularly when they were in distress. I had seen this on so many occasions.

There was one time when Shaun announced he wanted to go out dancing which shocked me. This was something he had never wanted to do before. It also put me on edge thinking about all the accusations he could put on me. Would he accuse me of showing my cleavage to impress other men or think I was trying to score one if he happened to see my eyes averted towards a man? I would absolutely need to watch my step at a venue with so many men around. When we arrived at the club, we saw a woman standing on her own crying. The woman was a little younger than us and very attractive. We stopped when we saw her as she looked extremely upset.

'What's wrong?' I asked her. 'Is there anything we can do to help?'

The woman introduced herself as Lily. She then went on to explain that she had caught her boyfriend kissing another woman. She pointed to where he was at the bar now talking with this other woman he had been kissing earlier. I felt so sorry for her as tears began streaming down her face.

When Lily thanked us for stopping to listen, Shaun said, 'Come over here with me for a second.'

Shaun then grabbed her hand and walked over to the bar where her boyfriend was standing. Right before my very eyes, he pulled Lily close and gave her a passionate kiss. I couldn't believe what he had done in front of me and what I had seen. My sympathy for Lily had just gone out the window as she totally embraced what Shaun was doing. She knew he was my boyfriend. Whatever happened to women sticking together? I ran into the toilet and collapsed into tears.

After about five minutes, Lily came in to see where I was.

'It was all an act, hun,' she said. 'I had to get even. Shaun was such a help and is so nice.'

When I walked back out into the club, Shaun acted as though nothing had happened. Wearing his winning smile, he gave me a hug. When I later tried to talk about what happened, I got told to 'drop it.' It never came up again. So much for being faithful to me.

On another occasion, his brother's girlfriend, Katie, got into a fight with his brother. I wasn't sure what the fight was about, but his brother got so angry that he cut her favourite skirt into shreds. We were about to go out for coffee when he invited Katie to come with us. Ordinarily, I wouldn't have minded, but it had been a while since Shaun and I had actually been out anywhere together other than the horrible experience at the nightclub. Over milkshakes, Katie sat there and told us how unhappy she was. I was stunned as Shaun told her how beautiful she was and how she could do much better than his brother. I didn't get involved in this conversation. If I made judgmental comments about Shaun's brother, I would certainly have paid for it later. What hurt the most was that over our conversation, Shaun and Katie were sharing a milkshake. They were behaving like a couple and that made me feel like the interloping third wheel. He then acted surprised when I told him how I felt later than evening.

'I was just being supportive, babe. The woman is family,' Shaun said.

He always managed to twist situations so that I looked jealous and possessive. Have I ever said how much I hated being called 'babe' by Shaun? I truly felt objectified by it.

It was always a one-way street with Shaun. He could

do what he wanted, whenever he wanted. But I could be doing absolutely nothing wrong and the accusations would commence anyway.

A prime example was when we went to Sarah's birthday party. My friends were eager to meet Shaun as they had heard so much about him. I'd only mentioned the good things, which lately were a very tiny proportion of his behaviour.

And so it was the following Saturday night that Shaun and I made our way to Sarah's parents' house for her celebration. When we arrived there, the dining room looked absolutely gorgeous. I could tell a lot of time had been spent preparing for Sarah's birthday dinner. As I had been to Sarah's parents' house many times before, I knew that what was laid on the table was their finest dinnerware. Shaun came to the party very prepared, dressed well as usual, carrying a large bouquet of flowers for Sarah. It made me so happy to see Sarah again and meet Sam. They made a stunning couple. When we sat down, Shaun stole the show with his friendly chatter. I started to feel relaxed as the man sitting next to me was identical to the Shaun I had first met. He was even talking to Alan which I was most nervous about after the incident of when we first moved in together. Telling Sarah's mum that her lasagne was the best he'd ever eaten won her over. The night seemed to be going particularly well until I started talking with Clyde. Clyde was a mutual friend both Sarah and I had known since we were children. I noticed Shaun's eyes darken and cloud over with suspicion as my conversation with Clyde continued. It probably didn't help that Clyde was also single and easy on the eye. The tone of Shaun's voice changed and he started to stare at me rather than pay attention to Sarah's party guests who surrounded him.

Out of nowhere, Clyde said to me, 'That's a great dress you're wearing.'

I didn't respond and instead tried to diffuse the situation by saying how delicious Sarah's birthday cake was before everything took a nasty turn. When it came time to say goodbye to Sarah and the crew, I knew that I would not have an easy night when we got home. In fact, Shaun was quiet for the entire car trip home, not uttering a word.

'Take off that dress,' Shaun said.

We had just walked in through the door at our place.

'Shaun, I just —'

Out of nowhere, Shaun backhanded me. My cheek stung but it didn't hurt too much, it was more his action that surprised me. Outright slapping me was something Shaun had never done. I went silent.

'Take off that dress,' he repeated.

All thoughts of having a quick shower and going to sleep quickly left me. Adhering to Shaun's orders, I slowly took off the dress right then and there next to our front door as he had requested.

'Now get outside,' said Shaun.

'You can't be serious. It's absolutely freezing,' I said.

'You should've thought about that before you started flirting with Clyde,' came Shaun's reply.

I was too tired to defend myself and knew that it would

make no difference. Once Shaun had made up his mind about something there was no changing it. I had learnt this the hard way so many times before. Slowly I began to step outside.

'I'm sorry it has to be like this, Carmella,' said Shaun. 'Things will change when you stop flaunting your body to every man in sight.'

So for the next half an hour I was standing on our doorstep wearing only my bra, underwear and stockings in the freezing cold weather. I felt like a pet dog that had been kicked out of the house for bad behaviour. I knew better than to start ringing the doorbell or calling for help. Ha! He certainly wasn't worried about me flaunting my body outside on this occasion!

Once I was let back inside, I gathered some stuff from Shaun's and my bedroom and moved into the guest room for the night. Just as I was settling in, Shaun opened the door to ask why I was sleeping there. I told him I wouldn't sleep with him because of how I was treated tonight. Shaun left, but not before throwing my dress at me on the way out which I had left on the floor by the front door.

CHAPTER 26
SCREENSAVER INCIDENT

One evening I heard a knock on the door. I glanced at my watch and it was almost 8.00 pm. This is odd, I thought to myself. We hardly ever got visitors, let alone this late into the evening. I for one wasn't comfortable having anyone I knew come over. Who knew what Shaun would say or do? Putting on a pair of slippers I walked over to the front door. A young woman who looked to be in her early twenties stood there wearing a miniskirt and midriff top. Her hair hung loosely over her shoulders and she was extremely attractive. In her hand she was holding a bottle of wine.

'Can I help you?' I asked the young woman.

She looked at me, her expression hard, almost judgemental.

'I'm looking for Shaun,' she replied. 'I'm Becky.'

In an instant I recognised the name. Shaun frequently spoke about Becky, saying she had had a crush on him for years. Becky threw Shaun a surprise party for his twenty-first birthday when he was in the midst of a break up with one of his ex-girlfriends.

'Is he expecting you?' I asked.

I couldn't help thinking that if a young guy were at the door asking for me that I would be in serious trouble, and especially carrying a bottle of wine. Shaun would either think I was having an affair with him or he was an ex-boyfriend of mine I was trying to get back with. Before Becky replied, I heard Shaun's footsteps as he ran to the front door. He shoved me out of the way as he greeted Becky.

'Becky, I thought that was you,' Shaun said. 'What a nice surprise and you have wine. Come and sit in the lounge room with me.'

Shaun then took the bottle of wine from Becky and handed it over to me.

'Pour Becky and I a glass of this,' Shaun said to me. 'I guess you can have one too.'

I walked into the kitchen feeling angry as Shaun and Becky headed into the lounge room. There was no way I was sharing a wine with these two. I smiled to myself as I imagined myself pouring Visine into the now-full wine glasses. I would've loved to be around as the pair of them had a bout of severe diarrhoea as the urban legend suggested. With this amusing thought in my head, I walked back to the lounge room. The laughter I heard as I got closer was extremely loud. What they could be laughing about, I had no idea. I found my answer when I arrived there. They were both staring and laughing at Shaun's computer screen which displayed a photo of me taken early in high school when I was extremely overweight.

'She looks hideous,' Becky said to Shaun as they both laughed.

The pain I felt as I viewed this scene was indescribable. Shaun knew about all the painful memories I had during this very difficult time for me. I felt so betrayed as there were so many stories I had relayed to him during our time together.

There was one time when I was standing outside a portable classroom waiting to go into an English class. I was in year seven and extremely overweight. I had absolutely no confidence, and not having many friends didn't help. Out of nowhere a male student, who was probably around year nine or ten, ran up to me and smashed all my books to the floor. All I remembered was a loud eruption of laughter from behind me. I turned around and there were about three or four other students laughing at me. I bent over to gather up my books trying to keep a smile on my face as I did so. The girl I was standing with didn't even offer to help me. All I remembered was her saying that what had happened 'wasn't very nice.' Thinking back, I couldn't blame her. She probably didn't want to be the target of bullying either which she would've been if she had come to my defence. I often wondered what happened to that guy and found myself wishing not very good things upon him.

On another occasion I was in a graphics class. I was not very good at drawing but took a liking to this subject. One day a girl from my class asked me if she could borrow my pencils. I remembered loving those pencils and was very reluctant to say yes. She pleaded with me and promised to give them back at the end of the class. I relented and gave them to her. Once class ended I walked up to her and asked for them back. She said she didn't know what I was talking about and that she didn't borrow my pencils. I didn't take this any further as I was already the object of ridicule and it was my word against hers. Who would believe me?

There was also another time when I was collecting books from my locker after school. A male student in my math class ran up to me with a piece of chalk which he scribbled up and down my back with. He kept on doing this until I managed to escape into the girls' toilets to examine the damage he had caused. I cried as I saw the graffiti all over my jumper. I found myself thinking that he must really hate me to inflict this kind of pain on me.

There were so many other examples including these which I had shared with Shaun. Swallowing up the pain building up inside of me, I walked into the lounge room to bring the wine glasses to Shaun and Becky. They hardly noticed me as I placed the glasses on the table and quietly left.

Later that night when Becky left, Shaun walked into our bedroom where I was reading a book.

'What did you think of Becky?' he asked me.

'I don't know her,' I answered, my eyes not leaving my book.

'She laughed at your photo,' he said.

I ignored his words, sending him silent vibes to leave me alone. Shaun obviously did not comprehend this because he kept on talking.

'I know you hate the photo but I think it's cute,' he continued.

My eyes remained glued to my book pretending he wasn't there which made Shaun so angry that he started to yell. Alcohol consumption always made his bad moods worse if that was even possible.

'Save your lying words,' I said, 'for someone who falls for your shit, as I certainly don't.'

Shaun stared at me for a moment, stunned. He then shook his head and smirked before he walked off. I didn't even try to understand what Shaun's facial expression meant. I was glad that he'd disappeared from my sight, even if only for a few minutes.

CHAPTER 27
AWKWARD SEXUAL ENDEAVOURS

Following the incident with Becky, mine and Shaun's sex life became next to nothing. It had slowly deteriorated as the relationship wore on. Towards the beginning of our time together Shaun and I had a very healthy sexual relationship. There was no planning for it and it would just happen naturally when it did occur. There would be early morning quickies, sex in the shower and there were days when we wouldn't get out of bed. Apart from what happened with Becky, there were also many other reasons for this. Firstly, Shaun and I were obviously growing apart. We were talking a lot less and there was no longer that feeling of comfort between us. I blamed Shaun's actions for this. How could I feel sexual towards someone when I was being constantly put down and treated so badly? Secondly, Shaun no longer initiated sex and when he did it felt forced. And last but not least, I did not want to. When it did happen I always felt horrible, used and dirty afterwards.

There was an occasion one morning when I was making coffee for Shaun and myself. Shaun was still in bed so I carried our mugs to our bedroom. I leaned over to give Shaun his coffee when I noticed him looking at my cleavage. My sudden thought was that Shaun would think I was wearing this top to attract the attention of other men. This one time however I was proven wrong. Shaun grabbed both mugs of coffee from my hands and placed them on his bedside table.

'Come here, babe,' Shaun said to me.

I obligingly got on top of Shaun as he had so desired.

'Far out, babe,' Shaun continued once the sex was over, 'you're beefing up.'

Feeling shocked, hurt and angry at the same time I quickly got dressed and walked to the kitchen. Shaun walked in not long after me.

'Aww come on. I didn't mean it like that,' Shaun continued. 'All I meant was I didn't want you losing that figure you've worked so hard to get.'

I doubt he was telling the truth. Lately Shaun always seemed to soothe an insult with an explanation.

This scenario did not change all that much the next time we had sex. I had finished having a shower and was headed to the kitchen to make dinner when I heard his voice.

'Come into the lounge room, babe.'

At the time I had no idea what he wanted but I made

my way towards the lounge room anyway. I walked in as Shaun was switching off the television.

'Babe, I'm horny, let's have a quickie,' said Shaun.

He looked incredibly worked up and desperate for sex. I didn't feel like it, but I was his partner so decided to go along with it. It was fairly quick, which suited me fine. Once it was over I went and prepared dinner as planned. Once Shaun and I had finished eating, Shaun announced that he was going out for a while. Ah, I thought to myself, the joy of freedom. I could watch whatever I felt like. Getting myself comfortable on the lounge, I switched on the television. What was shown on the television shocked the crap out of me. There on the screen was what appeared to be a paused picture of a porno DVD! I quickly ejected the DVD from the player. So Shaun was worked up over what he watched on the television and not me after all. Hypocrite, I found myself thinking. Whatever happened to the agreement of turning your face away from the screen when there was nudity? Feeling angry and used, I decided to watch *Sex and the City* that evening. This was one of the movies which would definitely have been on the 'banned' list. It was my way of getting payback for the way he'd treated me. Sadly, things were about to get even worse following this incident.

* * *

'I'm taking you away for the night,' Shaun announced one day. 'We're leaving tonight. Wear something nice.'

I was so surprised as it had been such a long time since we had done something like that. Pushing my suspicions aside I went along with it. I chose to wear a knee-length black dress and a pair of high-heeled stilettos. The dress was a little modest as the last thing I wanted tonight were issues with my appearance. Shaun smiled when he saw me which I took as approval. We called a cab and were on our way.

The Sheraton Hotel which Shaun had booked was very glamorous. When we arrived, there was a black box tied with a large red ribbon sitting on the bed.

'For you, Carmella,' Shaun said, lifting the box from the bed and handing it to me.

I opened the box and inside there was some very risqué black lingerie which included lacy underwear and a bra.

'For later,' Shaun said, leaning over to kiss me on the cheek.

OK, I thought to myself, go along with this and see what happens.

We ordered room service for dinner and were on our second bottle of champagne. By this time I was actually feeling relaxed and having a good time. I was definitely also tipsy. In the middle of our conversation Shaun suddenly got all serious.

'Why don't you go and put your lingerie on?' he suggested slyly.

Sure, I thought to myself. I slowly scooped up the lingerie and went into the bathroom to put it on. Eyeing myself off in the mirror I knew that I looked quite sexy.

This might be a new beginning for us. I wasn't sure if that was the alcohol talking or the way I really felt. Somehow I was pretty sure it was the former. My confidence was at a high when I walked out of the bathroom. This however changed in a split second. Shaun was setting up what looked to be a video camera.

'What is that for?' I asked Shaun with hesitation in my voice.

Shaun held my gaze for a few seconds before answering.

'I thought it might be fun to tape us doing it so we can look back at it any time we want,' Shaun said.

He didn't realise it, but right at that moment Shaun had destroyed any possible chance of us having sex. How could I even think about being recorded after what had happened in the last couple of instances we'd had sex? I couldn't possibly stand the insults if he called me fat or ugly when looking back at the video. Worse still, what if he showed someone or the chip got lost?

'No, Shaun, I don't think so,' I replied.

Shaun looked a little hurt but shrugged his shoulders and didn't push the situation. I couldn't help feeling a bit disappointed by the way the night had taken a turn for the worst. Why Shaun suggested something like this I didn't know. Nothing except sleep happened for the rest of the night. I felt like this was definitely the beginning of the end for our relationship.

CHAPTER 28
FAMILY DINNERS

Dinners at Shaun's parents' house became a frequent occurrence throughout our relationship. This was very awkward for me as I had to try and put on a happy face even though I wasn't happy with the way things were going with Shaun. To be perfectly honest, I dreaded being there. It wasn't only because Shauna was racist and didn't like me, but because Shaun had a habit of constantly leaving me alone at the kitchen table so he could go and play games on the computer. Not only did I not look forward to going there but they also gave me high levels of anxiety every time I had to attend. Honestly, it was always the same problem and person, Shauna. I would be burdened for hours about stories I had heard time and time again. I would have to act interested when all I actually felt like doing was telling her to be quiet. The issues were pointless, none of my business and plain boring. I, for one, would never have allowed Shaun to be put through this if it were my family.

There was one of many occasions when the bombshell had been dropped that we were going to Shaun's parents' for dinner that evening. Fantastic, I thought to myself, thanks for the warning. We had already spent an unpleasant afternoon arguing about a skirt I had purchased online and had arrived that morning. This particular purchase apparently outlined the curve of my buttocks too much. I was pissed off about that and now I had to sit through a dinner I did not want to be a part of. We got to Shaun's parents' house and Shauna immediately began talking about one of her sisters she had recently had a fight with.

'She tried to make a fool out of me,' Shauna said.

What apparently had happened was that Shauna had gone out to a wine festival with her sister, Brigid, and a friend. When it came to ordering their cheese platter and wine, Brigid had told her friend that Shauna didn't go out anywhere so knew nothing when it came to choosing a wine to go with certain foods. My first thought was that if this was the extent of your troubles, then you're doing very well. And, what makes you so special that you can have a drink without your husband but I can't without the presence of your son? Talk of this situation lasted for an hour when eating dinner and then another entire two hours when Shauna and I were the only ones left sitting at the table. I was so tired and aggravated, and the voice in my head screamed at me to just walk away. Of course

I couldn't as that would be considered rude. I felt a huge sigh of relief when that dinner ended.

The next thing I knew was that this pattern started to regularly occur. I'd become one of those women that everyone talked at and took advantage of. The same thing happened at the next family dinner also. Shauna was once again complaining about another sibling of hers who wasn't chipping in to provide care for their elderly mother. Again this lasted through dinner until Shauna and I were left on our own. The worst thing about it was that I heard Shaun having the time of his life in the next room on his Apple iPad which was his new and latest gadget. At that particular moment, I would've loved nothing more than to grab that iPad and stomp on it until it broke into a million pieces. When it came time to leave, I politely smiled and said goodbye to Shaun's family. I definitely needed to put an end to these situations. I wasn't sure how he'd take it when I told him. Shaun would have to be fairly blind to not know how I was feeling about what was regularly happening. I got my perfect opportunity to let him have it soon enough.

'Does it bother you if we have my mum, sister and her kids over for dinner tomorrow night, babe?' Shaun asked.

Silly question but easy answer. Saying 'no' would be my preference but how could I say that?

'OK,' I answered back. 'What were you thinking in terms of catering?'

'I thought I could order pizzas and that you could make one of your cheesecakes,' Shaun replied.

That seemed simple enough and not too taxing. I found cooking and baking rather relaxing.

The next day I let Shaun know that I needed the day clear in order to prepare the cheesecake. Shaun was pleased by this and seemed to understand.

It was around midday when I was busy preparing the cake that I heard the doorbell ring. I wondered who it could be. I was gratified to hear Shaun's footsteps making their way to the front door to answer it so I could continue with my cake preparation. The good mood I was in suddenly turned sour when I heard the sound of screaming which seemed to be getting closer to the kitchen area. Shaun then appeared with Beatrice and James. As usual, James glared at me with his evil sneer in place.

'I hope you don't mind, babe, but we have to look after Beatrice and James,' Shaun said. 'My sister had an appointment that she forgot about.'

My blood was boiling. Did Shaun not hear when I said I needed the day free? There I was for the next hour slaving away in the kitchen with two children following my every step. Obviously Shaun couldn't be bothered looking after them even though he was the one who had agreed to the babysitting. I was utterly exhausted by the time I had finished the cake. It did look brilliant though despite the two unexpected distractions I had. I picked up my work of art to put it in the fridge for later tonight. As I turned, my foot caught on something and I slipped. I fell to the ground, bringing the cake with me. I looked up and saw James looking down at me, a secret grin plastered on his face. The little shit tripped me over! Without saying anything I picked myself up off the ground and stormed into our lounge room. There, lying on the couch was Shaun playing on one of his stupid toys. He was so involved with what he was doing that he didn't even notice me walk in.

'Shaun, I have had it,' I said through gritted teeth. 'Your nephew tripped me over and the cake fell to the ground.'

'I'm sure he didn't mean it,' Shaun replied not even looking up from the screen he was so drawn to.

I then continued to tell Shaun I was sick of attending family dinners with his parents and over Shauna's whining. Shaun still did not appear to be listening. Letting out a piercing scream which sounded like a howl I ran to our bedroom, slamming the door behind me. I must've been sitting on my own for at least an hour before I heard Shauna arrive at the front door with her daughter in tow.

'Carmella, you will stop acting like a child and join the family for dinner,' Shaun said as he walked into our bedroom. 'You're complaining about a stupid cake when today my sister was seeing a lawyer for a divorce. Grow up. My mother is asking for you.'

Just like that Shaun once again managed to make me look like the bad person. Did the way I feel not matter to him? I think I had the obvious answer of 'no', especially with the latest arguments we had had.

After Shaun left, I did feel a bit juvenile for not making an appearance at the dinner right away. Nobody seemed to have missed my presence as I finally made my way to the kitchen with a fake smile plastered on my face. After a few quick hellos which came my way, conversation continued as if I hadn't entered the room. I didn't let my anger show as I saw James laughing to himself as he gobbled down his pizza.

After everyone had finished eating, Shaun, his sister and her children made their way to the lounge room to play games. Once again I was left hearing yet another tale from Shauna, this time about a friend who she feared had stolen money from her.

CHAPTER 29
ACCUSATIONS CONCERNING MEN

Accusations of being attracted, flirting with or staring at other men were a constant battle in my relationship with Shaun. In my opinion it was at the point of utter stupidity where there would always be some sort of issue every time a male was present. Sometimes I'd think to myself that if I was going to be accused of something, that I may as well do it. Of course I never did.

Dimmeys in Richmond was one of my favourite places to shop. The size of the department store was huge which meant you could easily browse around for hours and lose track of time. I, for one, could lose myself in this store, particularly when looking in the bargain DVD bins. This was one place I found that I was 'allowed' to go on my own with no questions asked. I wasn't sure why. Maybe it was because I always came home with multiple items to prove I had been there. It was surprising that Shaun never insisted on seeing my receipts! Lots of these included knick-knacks for our house as well as items for Shauna. I never stopped trying to get along with her.

Out of the blue one day Shaun surprised me by saying that he wanted to come along. Shopping around certainly wasn't his idea of fun. In the car on the way there he was chatty and in a good mood. Shaun told me how excited he was to be spending the day together. His mood didn't change when three hours later both our arms were filled with shopping bags. This was a first!

'I wouldn't have these if it weren't for you,' Shaun said pointing to a pair of Calvin Klein designer jeans which he'd been looking for everywhere.

When we got to the car to dump our bags in, I offered to walk to the parking meter to pay for our ticket. Smiling to myself, I was thinking it had actually been a nice day with no hiccups. I still had a smile plastered on my face as I walked back to the car. Just like that, Shaun's good mood was gone. I was disappointed, yes, surprised, no.

'I can see why you like it here,' Shaun said in a taunting voice.

'Why?' I quickly replied, eagerly awaiting what he had to say next.

Shaun made a point of looking around a few times before speaking again.

'Because of all the Wog men around here,' Shaun said. 'I think you're hoping that you can score one of them.'

Firstly, I hadn't even noticed the amount of European

men around and secondly, that remark was extremely racist. I guess he was Shauna's son after all though.

When he brought the subject up again a few nights later I found myself really angry by his ludicrous accusations.

'You're wrong, Shaun. I don't go to Dimmeys to check out 'Wog' men as you refer to them,' I said. 'If I wanted to be with someone else I would, so stop with the accusations.'

To permanently avoid the issue, I never went back to Dimmeys. This was another luxury I had lost.

Shaun owned a beautiful Porsche which was definitely his pride and joy. He named her Maddison. Lots of women I knew tended to get jealous of boys spending too much time with their cars. I for one certainly wasn't like that. If it kept Shaun happy and distracted him from arguing with me then it was the perfect solution.

One day after washing Maddison for almost two hours, Shaun asked me if I wanted to go for a drive. The weather was glorious so I eagerly agreed. Halfway through the drive I decided to wind down the window. The wind felt great blowing in my hair. I also put my sunglasses on as the sun was shining brightly. Life was good in that particular, short moment.

When we arrived home and pulled up the driveway I could see straight away that Shaun was unhappy. His sour look said it all. He was becoming more moody and unpredictable as the days went on. The thing that worried and scared me the most was how bad his mood could actually become. I better find out what the issue is, I thought to myself.

'What's up?' I asked Shaun.

'I'm not stupid,' came his reply.

To calm myself down I focused on counting the buttons on the stereo system in Shaun's car. Funny, I never actually noticed that they were navy blue instead of black.

'I saw you checking out that blonde guy in the car that pulled up next to us,' continued Shaun. 'That's why you like my car being clean. It gives you a chance to see men more clearly through the windows.'

I had no idea what blonde guy he was referring to and nor did I care. We could've passed one hundred men and I wouldn't have known. I also had never mentioned to him that I liked his car being clean. It amused me that Shaun actually believed he was onto something here. Sometimes I actually wished that I was as imaginative as him in inventing stories.

'The sunglasses were also a good cover,' Shaun pressed on. 'I'm sure you were having a good gawk at every Tom, Dick and Harry we passed.'

Shaun then came at me very quickly and my first instinct was that he was actually going to hit me. Instead he made a grab for the glasses I was wearing and angrily stomped on them when he got out of the car. He reminded me of an overgrown child as I watched him jump on them over and over. For the rest of our time together I was unable to, you guessed it, look out of my passenger window. As for the sunglasses, Shaun was the one who purchased them for me and I didn't like them anyway.

It was one Friday when Shaun suggested getting a

motel for the night. This suited me as it gave me a chance to abandon our place and, fingers crossed, avoid any arguments which we'd been having a lot of lately. We were lucky to find one at such late notice and decided on nothing fancy but instead something laid back and casual. I packed an overnight bag and also a few good movies, barring nudity of course, and we were on our way.

On the way to the motel we stopped to pick up Chinese takeaway to go with the yummy banana bread I'd baked the day before. That night we had an argument-free evening watching movies. Sex had evaporated from our relationship by this stage and no longer existed. I didn't remember falling asleep but we must've because the next thing I knew was that it was morning and I woke up in bed. We lay in bed for a while talking before I got up to have a shower. Dressed only in my bra, underwear and t-shirt I walked over to the bench beside the window to get my overnight bag before heading into the bathroom. There were a lot of voices and laughter coming from outside. It was Saturday so the place was bustling with guests coming and going.

Refreshed after having a shower, I walked back to where Shaun was pacing the room.

'Let's get the hell out of here,' Shaun said angrily, throwing his belongings into his bag.

I didn't argue. All my things were already packed so I was ready to go in no time. It wasn't until on the way back home that Shaun began to talk.

'You purposely walked to the window half-naked when you heard men talking out there,' Shaun said.

I certainly heard talking, but the blinds and curtains in our room were definitely closed. Hating the way Shaun constantly made me feel like a slut, I answered right back to him.

'I am getting sick of the way you accuse me of all these 'things' I supposedly do,' I answered back angrily. 'Go and get your head checked.'

There, I'd said it. He was a psychopath and needed help. Before I knew it, Shaun's hand came flying at the side of my head as it slapped me hard. Tears flowed freely from my eyes. I was crying more from shock and anger than pain.

'You get yours checked,' Shaun replied angrily, not knowing that, in fact I had a timely appointment with Ameera coming up in less than a week.

After that, the car was quiet for the entire duration home. I had to make this end I thought to myself, but more importantly what was the best way to handle it?

The appointment with Ameera couldn't have come at a better time. This one wasn't like many of my previous sessions had been. I had cried out my last tears of mourning for that relationship, and I wasn't going to waste my rage on a psychopath that I could see was beyond help.

While Ameera summed up my 'brain dump' of grievances regarding Shaun, I stared up at her in the hope that she could help me.

'So, let's review. Shaun is controlling. Shaun imposes conditions on you that he blatantly violates himself. Shaun is jealous of any interaction you have with the opposite sex while flirting with women himself. Shaun has done nothing to defend you against his family's antipathy, all the while professing his love for you. And, recently, he's graduated from emotional abuse to physical abuse,' she concluded.

Sighing, I nodded. Ameera put down the notebook she was cradling in her lap, and gave me her fixed stare.

'What are you going to do, Carmella?' she asked.

'I know what I should do,' I responded, 'but I am scared, Ameera!'

She nodded sympathetically.

'Men like that thrive on the fear they engender,' she replied.

I shook my head.

'No, it's not the fear of his violence or anything Shaun might do.' I paused. 'It's more the fear of the decision,' I explained. 'If I do this, am I going to look back and bitterly regret leaving, as a terrible mistake, years down the track?'

Ameera sighed and looked downcast. Then she looked up, piercingly into my eyes.

'The rule book says I shouldn't say this. But, no, I don't think you'll ever regret ending a relationship like this,' she concluded.

I felt extremely reassured and comforted by Ameera's words.

CHAPTER 30

FIGHTING BACK

The hitting started frequently not long after that incident in the car. It was never in front of anyone and always at home when we were alone. Shaun's strikes weren't hard enough to leave me battered or lying in pools of blood. The beatings shook me up but I never required medical care because of his violence. It was the cause of what was behind the attacks that struck home most which was that Shaun possessed an unnecessary, pathological jealous streak and wanted to take it out on me by hurting me.

There was one occasion when I cooked Mexican for dinner. I remembered I had spent a lot of time cooking this meal, particularly the tacos which were filled with top-quality meat and delicious vegetables. Shaun seemed to enjoy the meal and gulped it down in no time.

'That was a delicious meal,' Shaun announced. 'Your ex-boyfriend was Mexican, right?'

I had never had a boyfriend that was Mexican. I had no idea what the relevance of that question was but I was sure that I was bound to find out soon enough.

'Shaun,' I started to say, 'I've never had a —'

Out of nowhere, Shaun slapped me rather fiercely across the head.

'Come on,' Shaun said, smiling. 'You at least dated one and I bet you cooked this for him as well.'

Too stunned to respond, I sat there and rubbed the side of my head. I was truly dealing with a lunatic. Shaun got up from his seat and left me to do the washing up and whistled a tune as he wandered off. I so hated him at that point, wishing I had poisoned his meal.

Another time was when Shaun had a few of his mates over to watch the AFL Grand Final one year. There were about four of them all crowded around in our lounge room. As I recall, the match was extremely close and there was a lot of shouting going on as the end of the game neared. I was sitting at the kitchen table reading one of my true crime novels when I was summoned.

'Hey, babe,' said Shaun. 'Grab us some more beer from the fridge.'

Laying my book on the table, I walked over to the fridge, grabbed some beer and headed to the lounge room. Handing the beer over to the guys, I glanced at the TV and saw that there was only one point difference in the game. I wasn't into the AFL but this game looked so close.

I stood at the doorway to watch the remainder of the game, leaving as soon as it was over to give the guys their space. It had also occurred to me that Shaun might think I was trying to hit on one or maybe all of his mates.

Once his mates left, Shaun came into the kitchen where I was once again seated with my book.

'I thought you didn't like the football,' Shaun said.

I looked at him and replied that I didn't. I returned to reading my book when suddenly Shaun snatched it from my hands and flung it across the room.

'I saw you eyeing off the footballers' legs,' Shaun said. 'Are you perving on them because I've put on weight?'

It was true that Shaun had become a bit more rounded but no, I was not admiring the football players on the television. Sighing and feeling fed up, I tried to make him see reason.

'Shaun, I was merely tuning in because the game was so close,' I said.

Shaun slapped me hard across the face and told me never to look at men on the television or in person ever again. Where did that leave me? I thought to myself. Should I permanently strap a bandage across my eyes? I could still feel the sting of Shaun's slap as I was left alone with these thoughts.

Sitting there at work one day thinking long and hard about Shaun's recent physical violence, the email could not have arrived at a more appropriate time. It was from the Human Resources Department:

Dear Carmella,
Thank you for your email outlining your recent experiences concerning Luke Davenport. We have reviewed several other written submissions similar to yours and would therefore like to inform you that appropriate action has been taken. Luke is no longer an employee at Student Glamour.
Regards,
Human Resources

My heart almost leapt out of my chest with pure joy. I fought Luke and had actually won. I vowed to myself that the next time Shaun laid a hand on me that I would not allow it. I despised Shaun's physical abuse and soon got my opportunity to prove that I wasn't spineless.

It was one Saturday night and I was home on my own. I wasn't sure where Shaun was but being home alone was like gold to me. His moods continued to be unpredictable and I didn't know what to expect from him. I secretly referred to him as the 'Melbourne Weather Bureau'. Just as we could get four seasons in one day, Shaun could change moods four times over. I was watching *Wicker Park* which was one of my favourite movies. Horror films were my favourite but I had a special place for this movie since the first time I watched it. I was a big believer that what was meant to be would happen. This movie demonstrated that true love always won out no matter what obstacles were put in front of you. Lately however, I looked at my own life and questioned that.

Just as the end credits were finishing Shaun staggered

through the door. By the way he was moving I could tell that he had been drinking. I did not even dare question him about his whereabouts, nor did I find myself especially caring.

'What are you watching?' Shaun asked me.

'Wicker Park,' I replied.

Shaun looked at me with red, bloodshot eyes. It took him a moment to reply.

'Why did you turn it off?' came his reply.

His eyes stared into mine, which were full of accusations as usual.

'The movie just finished,' I said.

Shaun then walked up to me and pulled me off the couch. He threw me up against the wall moving his body in close to mine.

'You love Josh Hartnett, don't you?' he asked.

What was this man thinking? I had never even mentioned Josh Hartnett in all the time I had known Shaun. I was afraid as I didn't know how much Shaun had actually had to drink. Adrenaline was pumping through my body as I was unsure what Shaun planned to do next. I was up against a wall with no escape, not knowing what was going to happen to me. Was Shaun going to hit me? Or would he beat my head against the wall? Would I need to go to a hospital? It seemed like hours we were in that position before Shaun released me just like that and slowly inched away from me. Suddenly feelings of pure rage flooded inside of me. Was I destined to be this man's punching bag for all of my life? I was sick to death of this man and his threats. Shaun was still only inches away from me when suddenly, with all my might, I lunged towards him and pushed him hard. Shaun, not expecting this, fell forwards and toppled over. I looked down at him after he turned himself over and bore my eyes into his.

'What's your plan now? Are you going to hit me?' I yelled. 'You're a no-good woman-beater.'

Shaun stared straight back at me with a look of shock and maybe I even saw a tiny bit of fear in his eyes. This was the first time I had stood up to him and it felt great! First Luke, and now this. He then slowly got up, switched on the television and sat on the lounge like nothing had happened. Convinced he was not going to do anything else, I slowly crept out of the lounge room towards our bedroom. In that moment I was feeling totally scared by my own behaviour but victorious that I had fought back. Shaun's unpredictable behaviour was concerning but I had showed him that he couldn't do anything he wanted to me whenever he felt like it. For the rest of the night I felt as though I had the upper hand and genuinely believed I could slowly gain my life back.

CHAPTER 31

GASLIGHTING

The physical violence stopped after I pushed Shaun. I suspected this was because he was surprised by my courage in standing up for myself. It did make me feel good and not as frightened as I once was. Shaun, as I expected, did start up a new way of trying to torment me. I later found out that the term used for his new behaviour was 'gaslighting'. The meaning of this in the dictionary was, to *'manipulate (someone) by psychological means into doubting their own sanity.'* This was definitely something Shaun had been guilty of doing to me on a number of occasions.

One Friday evening we were at my mother's eating a quiet dinner. Out of nowhere, Shaun blurted that he had found out that I had gotten into a car full of men who were my mum's next door neighbours. The silence that followed this statement clearly indicated that neither my mother nor I had any idea what he was talking about.

'Come on,' Shaun insisted. 'The other night when you said you were coming here for a visit. I heard that it was a cover story so you could go out somewhere with the guys who live next door to your mum.'

The family my parents lived next door to were Spanish and they consisted of a couple, their three sons and two daughters. My parents were acquaintances of theirs and their relations only included a friendly 'hello' here and there as well as the odd Christmas card.

I barely knew them when living with my parents. There were maybe a couple of times I picked up one of the boys from school when I was living at home with my parents. This would've been quite a few years ago now.

'Shaun, that is crazy,' I said.

'I know you went somewhere but not sure where and I know you helped,' Shaun replied, pointing at my mother.

We both tried to defend our position. This was absolutely insane. I usually tried not to be argumentative in front of others with my partner but the situation was absurd. Why would I get into a car with a group of men that I didn't know? I asked Shaun who this supposed 'source' was that was feeding him this information. He refused to answer and stated that he did not want to give the identity of this person away. Shaun then announced he was leaving as he was starting to feel bullied. He really could behave like a child and I was glad that my mother had a full viewing of this also. It was on this rare occasion that we had come to my parents' house in separate cars. I advised Shaun I would be staying until I had finished dinner and he stated that I had his 'permission' to. Even if he wanted me to go home with him I don't think I would've. He politely thanked my mother for dinner and headed off.

When Shaun left we tried not to discuss what happened but it was difficult not to. It was at this point that I realised how much my mother felt sorry for me and she only had a glimpse of what I had to put up with.

'Are you sure you want to keep going with this relationship?' she asked me. 'Think long and hard about what you want and what makes you happy before you commit to anything further.'

I was grateful for my mother's logical advice but I didn't think she realised how difficult it was for me to up and leave this relationship. I also started to worry that I had become a little accustomed to this behaviour and that I was starting to think it was acceptable, despite Ameera's timely reality check. It was extremely hard for me to continue this conversation, so I finished dinner, hugged my mother and left.

I drove back home from my parents' house that night not knowing what mood Shaun would be in when I got there. Shaun was watching television when I arrived home and seemed happy enough to see me. I heard nothing of this again and found myself wondering if I had imagined the entire situation. Ordinarily, Shaun would never let something like this slide.

On another occasion I had just arrived home from work

extremely tired and all I wanted to do was rest. Shaun was sitting in the lounge room and I walked in to join him.

'I heard from your friend Linda Davies today,' he said.

I paused, thinking for a moment before I replied saying that I didn't even know someone named Linda Davies.

'She certainly knew you as she knew all about your job,' he said.

'As I said, I don't know her. How did she contact you?' I asked.

'Through Skype. Come here, I'll show you,' Shaun replied.

We walked over to the computer where he showed me his recent contacts and where Linda Davies was listed. Her profile photo showed a woman with short dark hair and glasses. I had never met nor seen this person in my entire life so I continued to reiterate this over and over again like a broken record.

'She told me you cheated on me. When I asked her the date of when you cheated I knew she was lying because it was the date of my brother's birthday party,' Shaun said. 'She also told me that you've been drinking when I'm not around.'

On his computer, Shaun pulled up some photos of me at my work Christmas party from four years ago. These photos were taken even before I had met Shaun. The thing I found absolutely bizarre about this was that these photos had all been on my Facebook account. Is it possible that Shaun had somehow reactivated my account and taken copies of these photos? In this moment I felt like I was going absolutely mad. It would be pointless to accuse Shaun of hacking into my deactivated Facebook account as he would flatly deny it.

Shaun put his arms around me and hugged me, advising that I may have some enemies out there. He also said he couldn't be around twenty-four hours a day to protect me. A chill ran up and down my spine when I heard these words.

For the next few days I started to think about people I may have upset without realising it. Maybe I did know a Linda Davies? She certainly didn't look familiar but people change their identities all the time. I began to worry, carefully watching how I treated people and looking over my shoulder every time I walked. Shortly after these incidents occurred I gave myself a harsh lecture. I made myself believe that I wasn't crazy but that it was Shaun, once again, playing with my mind.

CHAPTER 32
LAST CHRISTMAS

We spent Christmas Eve with both mine and Shaun's family that fatal year. I wasn't a huge fan of Christmas but knew it was an important holiday for Shaun and his family. Being from an Irish background they were very traditional and regularly participated in Christmas mass and cooking up roast ham.

The event was held at Shaun's parents' mansion. My mother was not very social so I was both surprised and delighted that my parents were attending. This made me feel less of an outsider as the majority of mine and Shaun's time was spent with his parents and family. The evening commenced with opening presents (another Irish tradition) and then dinner. Shaun's and my parents were eating inside and myself, Shaun, his brother Dean and girlfriend ate outside. Our parents had now met a number of times so were familiar with one another. Shaun was drinking heavily again which made me feel very worried. There always seemed to be more issues (if possible) when Shaun drank, and he was far from being a happy drunk.

As the evening wore on, Shaun's drinking only increased. I noticed him opening his second bottle of Jameson whiskey only moments earlier. He had a big fight with Dean who then decided to leave the dinner with his girlfriend. Dean gave me an apologetic look before leaving. He also knew what his brother was like after being on the booze. Shaun was definitely in the mood for an argument which left only me to do that with.

'Your mum and dad don't look like they're having a good time,' said Shaun.

How he knew this, I didn't know as we had hardly spent any time at all with the folks inside. The only thing I could possibly think of was that Shauna had been in his ear which would not have surprised me.

Shaun had an evil look in his eyes when he grabbed onto my arm. I quickly and roughly pulled away from him. There was no way Shaun would ever lay a hand on me again.

'Do they think they're too good for my parents?' he continued. 'Look at this beautiful mansion. How could you not be happy to be here?'

I didn't respond but instead walked into the house. I sat with mine and Shaun's parents for a while. Conversation seemed to be flowing rather nicely with a lot of chatter happening, particularly about family and grandchildren.

After about an hour my parents announced that they were leaving. I walked them to the car and Shaun followed close behind. At that moment, there was nothing more I wanted than to go home with them. The words screaming in my head were saying to go but they remained unspoken. I doubt I would've gotten my wish on this occasion and knew I had to face whatever awaited me.

'I hope you had a good time and I can't wait to see you tomorrow,' Shaun said to my parents.

I heard and understood the sarcasm in Shaun's voice but only I would've known this. We were having lunch with my parents the following day which Shaun would not be looking forward to. My parents told us they had a lovely time before leaving. I watched their car drive off and stood there until Shaun urged me to go inside.

As soon as we got inside and into the lounge room the verbal abuse commenced, worse than it had ever been before.

'You know you're a fat Wog bitch and that no one will ever want you,' Shaun said.

I looked at him, not saying anything and wondered to myself what I had done to deserve these insults this time.

'You're worse than useless. I hate you and your whole family. You're all shit,' Shaun continued.

I tried to leave the room but remembered being frozen with shock and not sure what to do. Shaun kept drinking more and more as further insults about me, my family and friends continued for hours. My head was spinning and not for the first time. I felt out of control to the point where I thought I was having a nervous breakdown. The situation felt so surreal to me that I thought I must've been in some sort of nightmare. At one point, Shaun's mother walked through the door and calmly told Shaun not to yell. He told her that the night was ruined because of my parents and the only reply she had was that she hoped she didn't have anything to do with it. The last thing I remember was looking at the clock on the wall to see that it was 5.00 am before I passed out from shock. The abuse had been going on for hours.

I woke up later on Christmas morning, around 9.00 am. Shaun was sprawled out on the couch, an empty bottle of Jameson lying beside him. What was I still doing with this person? The house was deathly quiet. My head felt so heavy and would not stop spinning. I got up from the chair I had slept in and slowly crept out of the room and downstairs to go to the kitchen. Shaun's father was in there making coffee. I actually liked Shaun's father as he was the only family member who seemed to respect me, although he was always very quiet. He had a worried look on his face which told me he was well aware of what had been happening last night until the early hours of the morning. He asked me if I wanted a lift home or to my parents' house. I declined this offer. What made me do this, I wasn't sure. I had no car, nor credit left on my phone, so I was now in an awkward situation. We were expected at my parents' house for lunch, so my choices were to catch the train there or wait. I decided to wait for Shaun which once again I had no idea why. That was so utterly stupid of me.

Shaun slept until 12.00 pm. He rubbed his eyes and asked me what the time was. I told him it was midday. He looked at me for a few minutes before speaking.

'I know something bad happened last night but I can't remember what,' Shaun said. 'All I know is that I drank a lot and said some nasty things.'

How did he not remember what he said? It was at that point I knew I had to urgently do something about my mess and this time mean it. What was I thinking being stuck in this horrible situation? I found myself getting angrier and angrier as I thought about last night's events. This had to be stopped and the only person who could do that was me. Ameera was right.

Shaun told me that he was too hungover to go to my parents' house for lunch. I told him I was happy to go on my own; I was quietly relieved he wouldn't be coming along. The drive back home in the car was deathly quiet. Neither of us felt like talking. As soon as we got home I had a quick shower and was out the door as quickly as I could.

In Shaun's absence, I felt like I could relax a lot more and be myself. The vibe was also chilled during lunch. It felt as though everyone was at ease and could speak freely with nobody taking offence to anything. We could even talk about the Richmond Coach being great, although I was the only one who knew of Shaun's offence to this. After lunch I sat down with my mum for a coffee.

'Is everything OK with Shaun?' she asked.

'He had a bit too much to drink last night and has a headache,' I replied.

I did not tell her about last night as I didn't want to worry her. When the time came to go back home, I found myself wishing that this afternoon never ended. I did however vow to myself that this would be the last Christmas ever with Shaun. This promise to myself provided me with great comfort.

'I feel a lot better now,' Shaun told me later when I arrived back at home. 'I spoke to my mum who told me that what happened last night wasn't bad. She said I was worrying for nothing.'

I rolled my eyes at this wretched and pitiful excuse for a man. His pronouncement was made without even asking me how I felt. It didn't matter what I thought. As long as I was in this relationship I would always be a prisoner to this man, abandoning my own life to him, and to some extent his family, particularly his mother. I was going to have to muster up the courage to escape this mess and promised myself that the sooner I did it, the better I would feel.

CHAPTER 33

COUNTLESS HOSPITAL TRIPS

Since that horrific episode at Christmas I started to stand up for myself more frequently with Shaun. I found the more I did this, the more vulnerable he became. Why didn't I try this sooner? Better late than never I guess!

The call came through about an hour into my dinner. It was Shaun. I was eating a lovely meal with my sister and nephew. The casserole my sister had prepared for us was fabulous. We were talking about movies we had recently watched or wanted to see. My nephew was talking about *Super Buddies* and how he would love to see it. I smiled to myself as children's films were not at all my thing but I told him it looked like a great film anyway. It was lovely to see his little face light up when I told him that I would take him to see it. I would make sure not to listen to Shaun if he tried to stop me from doing this.

Answering my phone was the absolute last thing I felt like doing. I picked it up with a heavy heart.

'Hi Shaun,' I said.

'Carmella, I feel sick again,' I heard Shaun say.

I stared out the window ahead which was facing me. What could I possibly do about it at this very moment? The last few weeks with Shaun had been extremely tiresome and challenging. Shaun's health had somehow drastically deteriorated for no apparent reason. The only thing I could think of was that Shaun did not know how to handle the new, outspoken me. There were countless trips to a number of hospitals with numerous medical issues. Some of these included eye, ear and stomach problems, as well as fatigue and vertigo. Tests taken during every visit showed that Shaun's health was exemplary.

'What do you want me to do, Shaun?' I asked him.

'I need to go to the hospital again,' Shaun said.

As well as me, some of Shaun's family members had also taken him to the hospital on one occasion or another. Most of the hospitals in our area now knew us and weren't in the least surprised when they saw us come through to emergency. It was actually becoming quite embarrassing.

'Can't one of your parents take you?' I asked.

I knew that Shaun was at his family's house for dinner this evening. His parents both drove so it made perfect sense that one of them should take him.

'They won't take me,' said Shaun. 'Nobody cares about me.'

I felt that this was definitely yet another guilt number. It was highly unlikely that anything was wrong with Shaun and this would be yet another wasted trip to the hospital. On the other hand, if I didn't take him I would be portrayed as being the worst person that ever lived.

'Fine, I'll take you,' I replied in a huff. 'Be at the front waiting or I will otherwise just beep.'

Shaun genuinely believed that his health was poor and would be clutching his stomach whilst shuffling through the doors to the Emergency Department. I was sincerely concerned about what these hospitals would think every time we visited. As the hospital visits increased, I found myself talking more and more to the doctors. The same questions were always asked about Shaun's current health and then the same tests were performed over and over again, with results confirming his unblemished health every time.

I could feel the moment we walked into the hospital that Shaun was in a foul mood. I wasn't sure if it was because I didn't go into his parents' house to say hello or if he honestly wasn't feeling well. As the days wore on, I found myself increasingly not caring. This might sound mean but it was true. I tried to ignore this as we sat in the emergency room waiting. Shaun and I hadn't seen each other that day as he was still sleeping when I left for work in the morning.

We thankfully didn't have long to wait and were called in to see a doctor rather quickly. Doctor Richards was his name. Shaun and the doctor ran through some routine questions and Shaun was then hooked up to a monitoring machine to check his heart rate. This was the most time-consuming part during our visits, other than waiting in Emergency, if there were a lot of people. When waiting in a chair by Shaun's bed, Doctor Richards had a few questions which I assisted Shaun to answer. Other than talk to Shaun and the doctor, it was nothing but a waiting game for me. After the monitoring was undertaken and a few further tests were run, Shaun was released. As always, the test results came back clear. I thanked Doctor Richards before we left.

The drive in the car on the way home was rather quiet. I didn't feel like getting into a conversation with Shaun right now. It had been a busy day at work and I was still peeved about my dinner being interrupted. It wasn't until we entered the house that Shaun spoke.

'So you wore that dress to work?' Shaun asked.

I stared down at my dress before looking up at him. It was a simple and elegant black pencil dress.

'Yeah I did,' I said. 'Why do you ask?'

'No reason, it's a bit short that's all,' Shaun replied.

I looked down at my dress again which was knee length and inwardly sighed. Shaun's remarks about the clothing I wore were becoming utterly tiresome. The criticisms as of late however had been coming through thick and fast. If I left the house in anything other than a tracksuit or jeans I was trying to impress someone. I'd given up on the idea of even trying to wear make-up as, according to Shaun, that was for single women or prostitutes.

'Shaun, it is knee length,' I said. 'Am I supposed to not wear any dresses?'

'You never wear anything like that at home, that's all,' Shaun said.

Not this again, I thought to myself. I absolutely felt like banging my head up against a brick wall. Shaun and I had had this discussion on so many occasions that I couldn't bear the fact of getting into it again. We hardly went out anymore and I did not see any point in dressing formally in the house. Shaun didn't agree with my logic and had resorted to calling me *Where's Wally* as I wore a lot of casual attire around the house, particularly striped jumpers. Before I was able to find the strength to respond, Shaun began to speak again.

'You were talking to Doctor Richards a lot this evening so maybe you wore that dress for him,' Shaun said.

I was surprised at the amount of fury I felt building up inside of me. Firstly, I had left a dinner early to take him to the hospital as nobody else would. Secondly, I had had this outfit on since this morning which was even before I knew I would be making yet another trip to the hospital. Shaun's statement was much too ridiculous for me to comprehend, let alone respond to.

'I'm going to bed,' I said.

Shaun was left standing there to stew alone in his own thoughts. I really did not care what he was feeling or thinking. It was about time I started to care about me and there was no better time than the present.

CHAPTER 34
MOTHER DEAREST

'Is that you, Carmella?' the all-too-familiar voice asked me. I found myself rolling my eyes and feeling surprised at the same time. It was my mobile you called, so who else would it be? It was Shauna.

My relationship with Shauna continued to be up and down and had been that way since the day we met. For starters, it took Shaun almost a whole six months to introduce me to his parents. To this day I still have no idea why. I found her to be a possessive and jealous woman, especially when it came to Shaun. She was also very stubborn and forever wanting her own way.

There was one time when I was looking for a computer for my parents. The computer they had was very old so they were in definite need of an upgrade. Shaun must've told Shauna about this as one day, out of the blue, we received a phone call from her letting us know she was at Harvey Norman. There was apparently a big special on computers and she wanted us to go and have a look. I wasn't in the mood but Shaun convinced me that we should go.

When we arrived at the store, Shauna was looking at a computer and was heavily putting me under pressure to buy it. The computer she was suggesting was of particularly bad value and expensive for what you were getting. I told her I didn't like it and wouldn't be purchasing it. The next thing I knew was that she was yelling at me in the store saying that I didn't have to like it and that it was supposed to be for my parents. You would think Shaun would've stood up for me then and there, being such an expert with most things technology-related but that unfortunately wasn't the case. There were a lot of customers around who were looking to see what was going on. I was so embarrassed that I ran out of the store in tears. Shaun told me that he yelled at his mum when I left the store but I didn't believe him. I ended up buying a computer for my dad's sixtieth birthday. Shaun also chipped in for the computer but told me not to tell Shauna that he did. He didn't tell me why but I suspected she would've got angry with him if she knew about this. She also reacted the same way when she knew other members of the family were helping anyone other than herself.

Another time was when Shaun and I visited his Uncle Dan's place for dinner. Dan was Shaun's father's brother. Dan was a Mormon and Shaun was interested in learning more about the religion. From a strong Irish background, Shauna did not agree with the beliefs of the religion and claimed she was a strong Catholic, just like her husband's entire family. She also said that Dan used it as a way to rebel against the family. We had a lovely time at his house and I found him to be very friendly and accommodating. I remembered his wife, Alicia, also warning me about Shauna, saying that she could be very controlling. This did not sit well with Shaun and I remembered him getting very defensive and denying this accusation. Shauna's attitude towards us was a little cool after we spent time with Dan and his wife. She didn't speak to us as much for a while and focused her attention more on her other children and their partners. I believe she became jealous of Shaun spending time with or becoming close to anybody other than herself.

Another occasion was when Shaun and I were having a nasty fight on the phone which involved him applying for a job. I had allegedly promised to assist him with updating his resume at 5.00 pm on the dot one particular afternoon. I couldn't remember saying that, so wasn't entirely sure whether to trust Shaun or my own judgement. On this afternoon I was tied up at work finishing a major project I had been working on for weeks. The project involved organising an event to assist students with disabilities which would raise money for their education and futures. My morale was high and I was extremely determined to wrap this up, as I felt like I was really making a difference in improving these young people's lives. I received a phone call from Shaun at exactly 5.00 pm demanding to know where I was. Hastily trying to finish this project, I responded by telling him that I would chat to him later. Out of nowhere I heard Shauna's voice in the background yelling obscenities which included, 'Fuck her!' and 'Dumb liar!' Truly and utterly shocked by Shauna's words and behaviour, I hung up the phone.

So much had happened between Shauna and I that I had always doubted that we could've had a strong relationship.

This was why I was amazed when Shauna called me on my phone that day. Shauna hardly ever called me and I didn't feel like talking. Yet, I answered and asked her what she would like to talk about and she let it all spill.

'I'm very worried about Shaun,' Shauna said.

I inwardly snarled and thought to myself that this was nothing new. If you were that worried about him, why didn't you take him to the hospital two nights ago, I felt like asking but didn't. I took a deep breath before responding.

'Oh yes, what about?' I politely asked.

'I know that he's been seeing a psychologist and that he's very unhappy,' Shauna said. 'This may be the cause of the medical issues that he's been experiencing.'

Shaun seeing a psychologist was news to me. I, however, didn't tell Shauna this as she already believed she had the upper hand with Shaun over me.

'I really need you to support him more,' Shauna continued. 'You are his life and without you he would be even more depressed.'

This was definitely a shift in attitude from Shauna. Most of the time she saw me as being a rival, or belittled me. I found myself thinking that Shaun obviously suspected that I was having second thoughts about our relationship and that he had discussed it with Shauna. This came as being no surprise to me as I suspected Shaun discussed a lot with his mother. I saw this phone call as being a tactic to ensure I stayed put in my relationship with Shaun.

'I'll do what I can,' I replied to Shauna. 'Although, if Shaun is so unhappy the best person to help him out of this is himself.'

I hurriedly made an excuse to Shauna and told her I had to end the phone call. Shauna began to cry but I didn't let this deter me. My main objective was to leave this relationship and to find the cleanest way to do it.

CHAPTER 35
DEATH THREAT

'If you ever left or cheated on me I would cut your clit off and leave you for dead,' Shaun said to me out of the blue.

Wow, that comment came out of left field. So, we were in the business of making death threats now, I thought to myself. I looked up from the book I was reading and into his eyes.

'In fact I'll even go one further,' he continued. 'I would also kill everyone you love.'

He had obviously figured out that playing the part of the wounded soldier wouldn't keep me around. This must be the new tactic of trying to keep me here in place. I didn't reply and I could tell that Shaun was very impressed with himself. He genuinely believed he had won and that I was planning to stick around. I didn't let on that I had already made my decision to leave him. That was for me to know and him to find out.

My acting skills were put into practice as I continued to play the part of being the 'happy partner'. The time was coming for me to tell him about our 'break' but not right yet. I wanted to feel safe and didn't want to rush things yet. Shaun's latest threat concerned me but not enough to put a halt on my plans.

There was one occasion on a Sunday night when we went to his brother's place for a barbecue. He had a new girlfriend whose name was Gina and he wanted us to meet her. Shaun continued his charade of being the supportive brother by accepting Gina into the family. I watched Shaun as he eyed off Gina throughout the entire afternoon. On our way home, Shaun commented on Gina's appearance which I believed to be another tactic to make me jealous.

'Did you check out Gina's hot body?' Shaun asked me. 'She really filled out that lacy top she was wearing.'

I found his comment extremely off-putting and disrespectful towards me but I knew I only needed to put up with Shaun's disgusting attitude for a little while longer.

It had been quite a few months since Shaun and I had slept together. When he announced that he had to go out that afternoon, I suspected that he may be seeing other women. Shaun had been out on quite a few outings lately with no explanation. He left on a Saturday afternoon and told me not to wait up. I was relieved to see him go as it meant not having to see his face or hear him for the rest of the day. I decided to give Sarah a call to fill her in on my plans to leave Shaun. After all, I would be moving back in with her. Sarah was ecstatic by this news but also concerned for my safety at the same time.

'Will you be safe once you spill the news?' Sarah asked me.

After the most recent death threat I was unsure how to answer that question. I had filled Sarah in on some of Shaun's obsessive behaviour and rules imposed on me but not his latest plan to cut my clit off. Sarah had been a great support as of late and I didn't get the 'I told you so' speech, which I greatly appreciated. As well as Sarah, I had also informed my parents that I would shortly be leaving Shaun. I was comforted by the fact that they had said their door was always open to me should I need it. They said they were relieved by my decision, not because of the things I had said but instead by some of Shaun's behaviour that my mother had witnessed. Sarah and I chatted for a bit and I hung up the phone with feelings of getting a new outlook on life.

I saw this as a good time to make an appointment with Ameera to tell her of my upcoming plans. Ameera and I had now seen each other on quite a few occasions and since that breakthrough session I began to trust her more and more. She truly was my heroine, and she also had a lot of respect for me when I revealed what had eventuated with Luke.

'Telling him you want a break is definitely the easiest way to bring this situation to an end,' Ameera advised me. It was good to get clarification that my way of thinking was right.

'Should I try and stay and give it another chance?' I pressed Ameera. 'Will I regret my decision?'

'As I said before, not at all,' replied Ameera.

What a quick response, I thought to myself. Aren't psychologists meant to maintain 'neutrality' and just ask you questions rather than take a clear position? That rule was certainly broken on this, and the previous occasion, and was the only issue on which I'd actually received a clear opinion.

As my session came to a close, Ameera asked me one final question.

'What was the main reason you stayed in this relationship for so long after you'd established it was toxic through our work?' Ameera asked, giving me her trademark fixed stare.

I thought long and hard and there were so many reasons for my decision to remain in a relationship I was very unhappy in. Mostly, because I was afraid of being alone. But also, because he may have revealed some of my deepest and darkest secrets to people. Because I had invested so much time in this relationship. Because I may never attract the attention of a man ever again. Because no man may ever love me again. Because I was afraid to leave him. Because I may meet someone who would treat me worse. Because he may come after me and never leave me alone. Because he threatened to kill me and everyone I love. I, however, didn't say any of these reasons.

'I haven't been ready,' I replied to Ameera. 'Not to this point. Just saying I was ready to end it, isn't the same as knowing in my gut that I was ready to take the risk and accept the sacrifices of what getting my life back might entail.'

Ameera smiled and knowingly nodded which let me know she fully understood. I walked out feeling refreshed and ready to take on the world. Was I really ready to take on Shaun? There was only one way to find out and that time was coming soon for when I put my words into action.

CHAPTER 36
THE BREAK

So my decision was made. I was leaving Shaun. Well, in my mind that was what I was doing, but as far as he was concerned, we were taking a break.

'This is sudden,' Shaun announced when I told him my decision.

His attitude made me laugh and feel angry at the same time. After all I'd been through, did he genuinely think he could keep me trapped forever?

'Not really, Shaun,' I said. 'Our relationship has been rocky for quite some time. I'll be temporarily moving back in with Sarah.'

Shaun suddenly looked angry. It was probably not my smartest move to tell him where I'd be but I figured that he'd find out soon enough.

'How did I know that she'd have something to do with

you leaving?' Shaun asked.

I sighed then looked at him before starting to speak again.

'Shaun, in case you had forgotten, it's my place that Sarah is living in so it makes sense that I move back there,' I replied. 'And before you try and stop me or threaten me again, I have told some people about your death threats. You would be the prime suspect if anything were to happen to me or anyone I am associated with.'

There, I'd said it. Shaun continued to look at me, his look of anger was now replaced with one of sadness.

'Come on, Carmella! I was joking,' Shaun said. 'I would never hurt you. You don't have to leave, you know. If you want a break, I can move out of the master bedroom for a while to give you space.'

How did he consider that to be a break? Not feeling at all tempted, I politely declined Shaun's offer. I saw this to be yet another one of Shaun's controlling tactics. As long as I was in his house he would know where I was at all times. Shaun was not impressed at all by my response.

'I'm going out for a while,' he announced, slamming the door behind him.

I breathed a sigh of relief. That was difficult but I was glad it was done. How and when to move my stuff was next on my list to figure out.

In case I had to rapidly flee the scene I had already safely stored my jewellery and other valuables either at my parent's place or with Sarah. It had been a week since I advised Shaun of my leaving. Throughout this time his behaviour had dramatically changed and he was back to the Shaun I first met. There were flowers and gifts left everywhere for me, which of course I ignored. I was not going to be roped back in by a false façade. I had frequently thought about leaving Shaun, but this was the first time I had actually taken concrete steps towards doing so. If I backtracked on this decision now it would most likely never happen.

The reality of me leaving sunk into Shaun when he saw me pack my stuff into cardboard boxes. There were boxes filled with my clothes, books and DVD collection. I figured the easiest way was to gather my stuff and to make two or three car trips to move it all to my place. Sarah offered to help but I advised her it would be easier if I did it myself. Shaun seemed hurt and extremely disquieted so I didn't want to push him to the edge of insanity even further. He was also so unpredictable which meant I really didn't know what he was capable of and what his next move could be.

It was early in the morning on the day I left Shaun's house. I was all dressed and showered for work when I realised that today was the last day I'd be doing that in this house. I was feeling excited and scared at the same time. I quietly walked from room to room for a last look to ensure that I had not left anything of value behind. My large dressing room table still sat in what was once Shaun's and my bedroom. Sadly, I had to part with this as it wouldn't fit in my car. I wanted to keep this move simple and hiring a company to move all my stuff would surely make the break-up look official. He'd already questioned why I packed my entire book and movie collection. My freedom, sanity and happiness were far more important. I had also left behind a lot of our shared purchases and gifts Shaun had given me. Shaun, who had already left for work that day, knew I wouldn't be coming back here tonight.

'How long will you be taking a break for?' Shaun asked me on my last night at his place.

I hadn't even left the house and the questioning was already commencing.

'I'm not sure yet,' I said.

'I wanted to know if you'd be back on the weekend so I can make plans for us,' Shaun said.

Last night was Thursday and today was Friday. Did this guy not comprehend what a break meant? It certainly was not for one night. I didn't respond to Shaun and provided very dismissive responses to his further questioning. At that moment I didn't want to talk and wanted to continue on my mission which was to leave.

Before heading to work that day I once again sat in Ameera's cosy office. I figured today would be timely to have another chat. Ameera now knew a lot of what had been going on in my relationship, minus the recent death threats. I believed that if Ameera knew I was in danger that she would have to report this to the Police and I didn't want that to happen. Here we were again sitting in that all-too-familiar setting now known as my safe space. Ameera was asking me how I felt about the events of the last week, particularly of that morning.

'I know that I've made the right decision. We've

discussed it so much. But I'm still scared at the same time,' I told Ameera.

It's true, I was feeling afraid. There were a number of reasons why, including not knowing what Shaun's next move would be, and also possibly being alone for the rest of my life. Would another man ever want me? I knew I didn't love Shaun, if I ever did. How can you love a man who puts you down, runs your life and changes you into someone you hardly recognise?

'At the same time though, I knew I couldn't work at forgiving or even loving Shaun,' I added. 'Too much has happened and I know if the relationship were to continue there would always be resentment.'

Ameera looked at me and I knew without her repeating it, that she believed that I was making the right decision.

Just before the session ended, Ameera asked if she could ask me one more question, to which I replied that of course she could.

'If you could do anything at all this weekend what would it be?' she asked.

I took a moment to think before I replied.

'I am going to go out and have a drink with a friend,' I replied and laughed.

This would be the first time I had done this since that night I had been caught with Sarah.

'Well, go right ahead. You're free,' Ameera said.

When Ameera said those words, I finally realised that I could breathe and was no longer a prisoner. I had freedom at last.

CHAPTER 37

HARASSMENT AND MORE HARASSMENT

'When are you coming back?' Shaun asked me.

I sighed. It had now been three days since I'd moved out of Shaun's place. To be honest, I hadn't missed it for a second. It didn't take me very long to get used to the taste of freedom and the life I once had. The only thing which kept my anxiety levels up were Shaun's constant phone calls and texts. I was not yet at the stage that I felt I could ignore them. It was purely out of fear of what he might do if he couldn't get a hold of me.

'You know I can't answer that yet, Shaun,' I calmly replied.

'But I'm missing you like crazy,' he said.

'Look, I have to go,' I said. 'I'm tired and I'm meeting

friends for coffee.'

'Which friends?' Shaun quickly replied.

I realised after I spoke that I probably should not have revealed my plans to him. Shaun's questioning continued throughout every phone call. I knew my absence would make no difference in him trying to run my life. He truly was like a dog with a bone.

'It's none of your business,' I replied. 'Nobody you know.'

'You can tell me,' Shaun replied. 'If you're tired you shouldn't be going out.'

'No, I'm not telling you and I can go out when I want to,' I said.

Whoever knew saying a few words out loud could sound so good? I was actually doing what I liked, when I liked. Shaun however did not relent with the questioning.

'Where are you having coffee?' Shaun continued to press on. He sounded anxious.

'Like I already told you, it's none of your business,' I replied. 'We are on a break.'

I tried to communicate these words in a more forceful manner. Shaun couldn't handle the fact that what I did with my life had absolutely nothing to do with him. If I wanted to stick it to him, I should've told him I was going out for a seriously boozy night. Although I did respond to his calls and texts, telling him my whereabouts was going too far.

'Please come back tonight,' Shaun pleaded.

The tone in his voice had now softened. He was

obviously trying a different approach hoping I would make a hefty return to hell.

'No, I will not,' I said.

Not on your life was what I was thinking.

'I truly want you back,' Shaun said.

He was really starting to sound extremely desperate now and it was very off-putting. I saw this as my cue to end the conversation.

'I've gotta go Shaun,' I said. 'Goodbye.'

I didn't give Shaun a chance to reply as I hit the end button on my phone. And it sure felt good to cut the psycho off.

Following work that day, I met up with my friend, Tara, for a drink. Tara was an old friend from high school who I had lost contact with when I started seeing Shaun. She was a great mate and I was so excited to be catching up with her. The bar we were meeting at was one of my old favourites and was only a short walk from where I worked. I was still revelling in the fact that I was able to walk freely and do what I wanted without looking over my shoulder. It may sound silly to some but those who had been involved in an abusive relationship would understand this. This was a feeling I would be happy to feel forever. Tara was waiting outside when I got there. We hugged before walking inside to grab a booth.

'I'm so sorry about your break-up,' Tara said once we were seated.

I had a long phone conversation with Tara a couple of nights ago, so she was well-informed of why Shaun and I were no longer together. It was very difficult to talk about some of the events which occurred during my relationship. There were some things I would never share with anybody, mainly out of sheer embarrassment that I had allowed myself to be treated so badly for so long.

'Things happen,' I replied. 'You never really know who someone is until time passes.'

Tara understood that more than anybody. She, herself, had had a horrific relationship experience at one time. Her ex, Steven, was in everybody's eyes the perfect man as he was charming, intelligent and charismatic. The physical abuse started very early on in their relationship and lasted for two years. Like me, Tara hid a lot of what was going on until one day he nearly left her for dead by beating her up so badly. With the assistance of supportive family and friends, Tara was able to get a restraining order put on Steven, and leave. It felt reassuring to have a friend I could identify with and vice versa.

'You really need to start ignoring his calls and texts,' Tara said. 'It's the only way he'll understand that by 'break', you mean a permanent one.'

That all sounded very scary to me. I had filled Tara in on all the calls and texts I was still getting from Shaun. Maybe Tara's right though, I thought to myself. I should start giving Shaun a bit of the silent treatment.

In spite of my plans to avoid Shaun, the calls and texts started to rapidly increase. He called several times a day and sent numerous texts day and night. He talked about what we would do when I finally came back to him.

Surely he must have known that I didn't plan to ever come back? In almost every situation a break meant that it was over. I was certain it was common knowledge. Why would anybody want to take a break in a relationship they were happy in? I decided to take Tara's advice and ignore Shaun's constant harassment. That was when I started to notice his car frequently drive past my house. I locked all the doors and closed all the blinds when I saw this happen. We also made a point of having Sarah's car parked behind mine when we were both home so Shaun knew that I wasn't home alone. My parents had also seen his car drive past their house and also at my dad's place of work. Every once in a while he parked at the front of my place and sat and stared in. This I found extremely creepy as I didn't know how long he'd sit there for or if he'd walk up to the door and ring the doorbell.

Then one day something even more disturbing occurred. I was coming home from work on the train, I got off and walked over to where my car was parked at the station. Sitting on the driver's seat when I arrived at my car were two chocolate muffins in a white paper bag. These were the muffins Shaun used to buy me when we first got together. The difference was that these ones had smiley faces made out of Smarties. I wasn't sure what freaked me out more, the fact that Shaun had been in my car or the bizarre addition of the smiley faces on the muffins. Was this the first time he'd been in my car? Had he bugged my car? I wouldn't know what to look for if he had. Were the muffins poisoned? I didn't intend to find out so I binned them as soon as I got home. Who knows what would've happened if I ate them? Surprises were unpleasant at the best of times, let alone nasty or unexpected ones. I really needed to figure out a way to stop Shaun's behaviour. My problem was finding the best way to do it.

What I didn't know was that things were going to get a lot worse before they got better.

CHAPTER 38
THE END ... HOPEFULLY?

Shaun's harassment continued over the next few weeks. My plans of ignoring Shaun were thrown out the window when he began calling from an unknown number. I unfortunately needed to respond to these as some of my family members and friends had private numbers.

One night, I was about to go to bed when my mobile rang and startled me. It was almost 11.00 pm.

'Why hello there,' came the soft, all-too-familiar voice which sounded almost joyous.

I peeked through the curtain of my bedroom as I'd grown accustomed to seeing Shaun sitting outside my house.

'You're about to go to bed aren't you?' Shaun pressed on. 'This is generally your bedtime. The famous 11.00 pm.'

'Please stop calling,' I said.

I didn't bother to ask what he wanted as I didn't care. It was really proving difficult to get Shaun out of my life, but when I made the decision to leave our relationship, I was fully aware of how challenging it would be.

'I just wanted to hear your voice and know that you're OK,' said Shaun. 'Bye for now. You can't scare me off. I'll be in touch.'

That phone call, like all of them, left a nasty taste in my mouth.

Unfortunately for me, Shaun's actions didn't start and end with phone calls to me. Shaun also started calling my family and some of my friends. I never gave Shaun the contact numbers of my friends so I wasn't sure how he managed to get these. This started to annoy and also frighten me. He would enquire about my whereabouts and where I generally hung out. I warned as many friends and family members as I could, asking them not to reveal any information to Shaun about me. My mum advised that he had called her on many occasions pleading her to talk me into taking him back. This of course wasn't her decision and she rightly told him so. He then started accusing her of having something to do with the break-up and that it was what she wanted all along. My mum is a fairly strong woman, so she had gotten into the habit of hanging up when she heard his voice. Also, he wouldn't dare go near my parents' house. Their big doberman would make a meal out of him!

As well as on my mobile and to other people, the calls also commenced at work. One day I'd just arrived back at my desk after a meeting, when my phone rang. Surprise, surprise, it was Shaun.

'I'm ringing to say goodbye as I am about to kill myself,' he said. 'I really wanted you to know how much I love you and how I valued our time together.'

Shaun hung up the phone before I could even respond. I started to feel slightly guilty about not at least talking to him which I knew was exactly what Shaun wanted. He didn't answer his phone when I tried to ring him back. This behaviour was so typical of Shaun but I didn't want to be the only person who knew of Shaun's suicide if he did go ahead with it. There was no doubt in my mind that this was yet another attention-seeking act. I felt I had no other choice but to call Shauna. Her emotions certainly got the better of her when I told her about Shaun's recent threat to himself.

'Oh my God!' Shauna cried. 'Not my boy!'

The phone then went dead. Oh boy, did she not even know her own son? It was about an hour or so before I got an angry phone call back from Shaun, this time on my mobile.

'How dare you call my mother,' Shaun said. 'She was so worried.'

'Well, next time don't behave like such a baby,' I replied. 'And stop calling me.'

I hung up my mobile and switched it off. That was the last time I would be falling for one of Shaun's ridiculous charades.

Nothing prepared me for what happened next. I was

arriving home from work that same day when my mobile rang. It was an unknown number and I picked it up.

'You're alone aren't you?' I heard Shaun's voice.

I felt the anger rise inside me as I told him that I wasn't.

'Come on,' Shaun said. 'I only want to talk.'

Unlocking the front door of my house, I walked in and went straight upstairs into my bedroom.

'Shaun, just leave —'

I stopped dead in my tracks and almost dropped my phone as soon as I saw Shaun lying on my bed. My breath caught in my throat and my heart began to pound with what felt like ten thousand beats per second. How did he get into my house? I was the last one to leave this morning and I always made sure to check that every door and window in the house was locked. Think straight, Carmella, I told myself. Panicking and showing Shaun I was scared was the worst way to handle this situation. I stayed calm and forced myself to smile at Shaun. Taking a deep breath, I began to talk.

'OK, let's go into the kitchen,' I said to Shaun. 'I'll make us some coffee.'

Shaun smiled as he followed me downstairs into the kitchen area.

'Your place looks great,' Shaun said, walking around the kitchen.

I saw the scowl on his face as he examined the photo magnets on my fridge. There were photos of Sarah, myself and some other friends all smiling and holding up flutes of champagne. This gave me a strong sense of satisfaction, even though at that very moment I was shit-scared.

'Yeah it's pretty comfortable,' I replied. 'Take a seat,' I continued, pointing at the kitchen table.

I slowly began taking out mugs from the cupboard and turned the coffee machine on. The loud sound of it gave me time to think. I was willing Sarah to come home, as this was the time she usually arrived back from work and she hadn't mentioned going anywhere afterwards. Once the coffee was ready, I took the mugs over to the table and took a seat opposite Shaun.

'Thanks for talking to me,' Shaun said.

I had no other choice, I thought. You were in my house and lying on my bed. My main objectives at this point were to be calm, cooperative and appear interested in what Shaun had to say.

'I'm also sorry for breaking into your house,' Shaun continued. 'It's the only way I knew how to get your attention.'

It was no excuse and I had no choice but to continue listening.

'This is going to sound silly, but I treated you the way I did because I love you and never wanted to lose you,' Shaun said. 'You're the best thing that has ever happened to me.'

Shaun looked at me from across the table and I could tell he was waiting for me to talk. I tried to think of something which I hoped would keep the conversation going.

'You had a lot of rules for me to live by, Shaun,' I said. 'I couldn't do it anymore. The whole relationship was getting to me, especially not being allowed to see anyone. Why did you do it?'

This really got Shaun talking as he went on to explain how difficult his childhood was and how obsessive a lot of his ex-partners were, only some of which I knew about when we were together. I was so engrossed in listening to Shaun that I didn't even notice Sarah and Sam walk into the kitchen. As engaged as I was in Shaun's life stories, I couldn't let this deter the outcome of this situation which impacted my whole life. I wanted Shaun out of my life, permanently. When everyone noticed one another, the room went silent and still until I spoke and fixed Shaun with my most steely glare.

'Shaun, please, I am telling you this once and only once. Please leave my house, don't ever contact me in any shape or form and if you see me anywhere please ignore me and pretend you don't know me. I will have a restraining order put on you and if that doesn't work I will finish you off myself,' I said.

Shaun kept his gaze fixated on mine.

'I know you still love me and want to be with me,' Shaun said, his glance never leaving mine. 'You don't want to lose me.'

How could I not want to lose him? How could I possibly love someone that wanted to own my life?

Our gazes continued to be locked.

'Leave,' I said. 'And by the way, Shaun, I never loved you.'

These were the last words Shaun heard from me. Shaun left his seat at the kitchen table and slowly headed to the front door. On his way out he turned to look at me and I could read defeat in his gaze. An unexpected wave of emotion hit me and I broke down in tears. Sarah ran over to me and pulled me into a giant hug. My tears soon turned into hysterical laughter. I had beaten Shaun and it felt great to be the winner.

EPILOGUE

It had been six months since my relationship with Shaun ended. I still received phone calls and texts from him advising me that he desperately needed to finish telling me his story. His behaviour was non-threatening which made me believe he clearly wanted to explain some things. I didn't answer his texts but I responded to his calls as they still always appeared from an unknown number. Shaun knew better than to up his level of antics and try to further intimidate me. He had been advised time and time again that if anything were to happen to me that he would be the prime suspect. I tried my hardest not to let Shaun's behaviour get the better of me but it was sometimes rather difficult. 'Just give up,' I felt like saying. Perhaps if the calls and texts were rare I would find it in me to listen to him. His story was getting quite interesting before Sarah and Sam appeared. I still spent some of my days wondering if I would hear from him or not. If he did decide to one day cease the contact I would never know what happened to him. Shaun could be so erratic. My number had been changed twice in the last few months but Shaun somehow managed to find out what it was. Even though I was pretty sure I was OK I did still worry about my safety and the safety of those around me.

I often dwelled on the years I spent with Shaun and saw them as lost years. I wasn't saying that it was entirely his fault because some of it was definitely mine as well. I should not have stuck around and put up with his behaviour for so long, but I did. Allowing it to happen was like an endorsement for Shaun, making him think it was OK to treat me that way.

Finding the strength to leave and say no to Shaun was the most exhilarating thing I could ever have done for myself. I was so proud of myself for finding the inner strength that existed in me all along. It was not until I had left that life, that I realised that I had been poisoned, manipulated and humiliated. He had taken so much from me but I didn't let him take it all. Now, my life was once again mine and it felt like heaven.

TEN YEARS LATER

I looked into the fridge to see what I was going to make for dinner.

'I'm hungry, mummy,' the little voice beside me murmured as I felt a tug on my skirt.

I bent down to kiss the locks of thick, curly hair and smiled. Children sure complicated life but I would not have it any other way. Now married with two children, Aurora aged six and Raff, two, I couldn't be any happier. Finding some steaks, I turned on the stove and located a frying pan in my very full pot drawer. Just then, the doorbell rang. Aurora, who loved answering the door, ran to see who it was. I had warned her on many occasions not to do this but she still did. I smiled to myself and silently admitted that I was relieved to see her growing up so headstrong. She was certainly the child I had wanted to be, but unfortunately wasn't. Destroying her confidence was something I wouldn't do regardless of the consequences.

Both her father and I agreed on this sort of upbringing. I continued to prepare dinner but stopped to listen as I heard Aurora talking to somebody and giggling. It must be one of the neighbours, I thought to myself. Turning the stove off, I picked up Raff and walked to the door to check what was going on. I was not prepared for what awaited me when I arrived at the front door.

'Mum, it's your friend Shaun,' Aurora said, smiling. 'He was telling me that you were friends a long time ago and how much I remind him of you.'

I was frozen in shock and my legs began to tremble. Raff was in my arms wriggling to get free but I continued to keep a firm grip on him. I could not believe that after all these years Shaun was standing at my door. To my dismay he had not changed a bit except that he looked a tad older. His blonde hair was slightly grey and he was unshaven. Same blue eyes and cheeky grin. What the hell was he doing here? Thoughts of the past began to flood my mind, and they were all bad. Being banned from doing things. Feelings of entrapment by being isolated from all my friends and family. Not knowing how to leave and when I did, the constant wondering if I was safe. Shaun finding me, after all these years, told me that he may never have stopped tailing me. Had he known my movements for the last ten years, or had he tracked me down recently? My husband was away for the weekend, which left me wondering if he purposely chose this weekend to arrive here?

'Mum?'

I looked down at Aurora who was staring at me, a puzzled look plastered on her beautiful face.

'Are you OK?' Aurora continued. 'Why aren't you saying anything?'

I put on a brave face for Aurora before I spoke.

'Yes I'm fine, Aurora,' I replied. 'I would, however, like for you to take Raff to watch some TV while I speak to Shaun.'

Aurora looked at me with disappointment in her eyes.

'But mum, I want to speak to Shaun,' Aurora said. 'I even invited him to stay for dinner.'

Aurora gave me a look of triumph. This is what a confident child does. They do what they want without a moment's hesitation. At that moment, I gave Aurora a look which I didn't impose on her very often. She knew enough to listen to what I'd just said. Aurora reluctantly did what she was told and took Raff into the lounge room to watch some television. She gave me a cold stare on the way there.

Now here I was, ten years later, standing face to face with Shaun. By this time, I didn't have any interest in talking to him and wanted him to leave. Reaching for the door, my intention was to slam it in his face. Shaun however had other plans and stopped the door from banging with his foot. He gave me a piercing stare, one I had not seen in many years, but one that had haunted me the entire time.

'Carmella, the time has come for you to hear my side of the story,' Shaun said.

His look meant business. I had no choice but to listen.

Lightning Source UK Ltd.
Milton Keynes UK
UKHW010636050722
405403UK00001B/143